HOTEL SARAJEVO

HOTEL SARAJEVO

JACK KERSH

TURTLE POINT PRESS

NEW YORK

TURTLE POINT PRESS

Copyright © 1997 Jack Kersh

Design: Christine Taylor
Composition: Wilsted & Taylor Publishing Services

ISBN: 1-885983-21-2
LIBRARY OF CONGRESS NUMBER: 96-060921

For Sabrina,

who not only was born beautiful,

but, what's more, remains so

PART
ONE

AGAIN THE RAIN. Always the rain. Even though the winter has gone, there is still the rain. Following me. It followed me from our flat in the district, along the dead streets over the silent Miljacka with its sluggish waters that divide the city, then past the Central to the Sarajevo.

I have come to wait for Luka. The rain waits with me. It makes a sound like drumming on the good window, and splatters fitfully through the other, broken one.

Other than the sound of the rain, everything is quiet now. The Jevos are out scavenging for food, or whatever they can find. Once they brought back a '50s jukebox on a handcart. Though the front was slightly smashed in, they set it up proudly in the lobby, a trophy of war, and, even silent, it lent a majestic air to the old Sarajevo. Luka danced in front of it, offering Sandra his hand, which she accepted tentatively, as befits a princess.

The Princess Sandra. She's in one of the better rooms on the side near the courtyard. That's for protection in case of shelling. Almost always if a shell hits, it's on the outward, street side, so that there the Sarajevo looks like

3

HOTEL

a heavily pocked-marked face, but inside the court the rooms are still quite good and warm.

A tree still grows in the courtyard. It's a sycamore, large. One would think all the names carved in it would have killed it long ago, but somehow it's managed to survive.

The names are all there. Luka and Sandra, Nenad and Dejan and Jasmina, even Milorad and Ilija and Adnan and Maud. Some were quiet and went away. Others have stayed but I don't really know them all well—just the names and the faces that go with them. It's better that way. Some have real families and some only make believe ones, but all seem to prefer the company of their own kind here at the Sarajevo.

There're usually twenty to thirty of us. It changes. We're allowed to have friends from outside the Sarajevo, but only if they don't interfere with things as they are here. To actually *become* an Jevo you have to pass Luka's inspection. As he's moody and nobody knows exactly what his requirements are, we're a motley group.

My name is there on the tree also: tiny, almost unnoticeable—Alma. I like the sound of it. A princess could have a name like that. But I am not a princess. I am plain. I've always been plain. I must have been born plain. With straight, mousy hair, thin lips, and a nose that's not quite right. I think I'll have large breasts one day, but they're only just beginning. They feel like buds, and sometimes they hurt from growing.

Once when we still had water, Milorad saw me in the

shower and his eyes got big. Now he likes me. I like him liking me because he's the first who has, but I don't like him.

Maud is the only name on the tree that is not a Sarajevo but a Central. She is only twelve but already beautiful, with long dark hair and magnificent eyes. And she's never been raped. Luka wanted her to be an Jevo, but the answer from Vladan, the Centrals' chief, was no.

The Sarajevo is on the Maršala Tita and the Central is only on the Ulica Zrinjskog. Luka says we are better than they for being on a wider, more important street. However, they are fortunate to have water and, sometimes, electricity. I was there once before the war when Mother went to visit a friend. I waited downstairs in the lobby until I became bored. Then I wandered around, and Mother was angry when she found me staring at the well-dressed diners.

I was only raped once. The soldier was rough but not violent, and seemed to do it not because he wanted to, but because that's what soldiers do. The backs of his hard hands were hairy, and he had a scar on one at the wrist.

It was once when we went to Zuc for firewood and I wandered away from the others. Afterwards I did not cry, but merely straightened my dress and returned to the others silently.

I was not afraid. I'd seen Mother once in the little flat with Saša, and after that I knew what the sounds were about and they didn't disturb me as I went on reading.

I have only one book, *The Catcher in the Rye*, but because of it I speak English well. I think if I were not in love with Luka, I would be in love with Holden. Such a strange name. I wonder if he could love an Alma. Perhaps when my breasts are larger. Once I saw Luka and Ilija stare at a movie poster of a woman with big breasts, and how they laughed and joked and seemed to enjoy it. Milorad, however, looked away. Though when I was in the shower, he didn't look away. He kept his eyes on my breasts but wouldn't drop them to the other, like breasts were clean and that was dirty.

I felt good that he looked at my breasts and would not look at those of the woman on the poster. But perhaps it was because she was foreign and that made a difference.

I've never felt a need to stare at breasts or at boys either. I want to give myself to Luka, but only because I love him and he would expect it.

He's still not had the Princess Sandra. For that I'm glad. She's twelve, a year younger than me. But, unlike me, she's never been raped and so is clean like Maud.

Luka is the chief. That's why he requires cleanliness. I wish I could make myself clean for him so he would want me, but I'd still be plain, so perhaps he wouldn't even then.

All the same, I come here to lie on his mattress and pretend to wait for him, as I've seen Mother wait for Saša. Like her, I raise my skirt to the middle of my thighs so I can feel the cool air running between my legs like fingers. If they were Luka's fingers they would not be cool but hot.

I am not frightened to think about his fingers touch-

SARAJEVO

ing me. On the contrary, the idea excites me. Closing my
eyes, I can almost imagine it's him.

There's the sound of a shell exploding outside, but it's
far away and causes me to jump scarcely at all.

Once, in the night of a heavy shelling, we all sat together on the floor of the lobby, joining hands and imagining the noise as music. We sang or hummed along with it.
Then after a long time the sounds went away without
harming us, as though we had made a friend of them.

It's different, however, with the snipers' fire. All
the intersections along the Miljacka—that people must
brave every day—have warning signs that say, "Beware!
Sniper!" Still, it's as though the shots don't exist because
you'd be dead without ever hearing them. It's hard to
make friends with that.

Even before the fighting I had few friends. I'm quiet
and keep to myself, reading or thinking mostly. Here I
still don't have many friends, but I'm accepted as a Sarajevo and so am tolerated. It's true I'd like to talk to Sandra
to learn her secrets, but, really, other than my friend Jasmina, the few other girls here are silly and bore me.

As I lie here quietly pretending to wait for Luka, I
imagine myself as the Muslim woman lying dead in the
arms of her Serb lover. All Sarajevo is talking about it.
They were shot down while trying to escape. All day they
lay there, arm in arm, until some commandos rescued
them. Now they're on display in wooden coffins in the old
Town Hall.

Luka and I will never be like that, I'm sure. I'm going

7

to ask him to take me to see them when he comes, though he'll probably want to take the Princess Sandra as well. I don't think about being jealous. She has her place, as befits her beauty, and I have mine, though I'm not happy with it.

I was never happy with Mother, even before Saša, who was nice to me and sometimes played games with me. Once we played jacks on the floor and before I knew it we were both laughing out loud, so he was almost like a father to me.

I don't remember my father, not well anyway. I only remember we'd play a game and I'd hide under the bed covers, waiting for him to find me. Mother said he was some sort of factory worker, not intelligent or well-bred.

One day he apparently just tired of us and didn't come home at all. Mother said she never missed him, only the little extra money he brought. Then there was Saša and she didn't even miss that. Saša always brings sausages or bread to help out, and I've seen him hand Mother money, or put it on the dresser near her bed. I don't think it's just because she lets him do it with her. We're his family, he says.

Once he brought a radio and proudly set it on the kitchen table and then danced with Mother while I watched. He was a little drunk, and when he danced with me he held me close so that my breasts pushed against him, and his hand dropped to my bottom and gave it a pat. Then, when Mother was in the other room, he held the

wine bottle to my lips for a long swallow, pulling it away
laughing and replacing it with his lips on mine while the
wine was still in my mouth, so that when I did swallow, it
had the taste of him too. It was a heavy, sweaty taste that
I didn't understand. Yet it didn't disturb me. I only wondered why he would want to kiss someone so plain, and
that was what I was thinking when Mother came back
into the room with her face all strange. When he saw her
face he quickly removed his hand and pushed me away,
which I didn't like.

Later that night as I lay in the dark I listened to them
arguing for a while, though I couldn't make out the
words. Then there was the sound of a slap and after that
the usual sounds. Only this time I didn't close my eyes
and go to sleep immediately but, still in my dress, reached
a hand to feel my bottom as Saša had done, to find what
satisfaction he could take in having it there. Although I
was pleased at the round softness of it, I still couldn't
figure it out. Finally I decided it was because of the silky
feel of my dress. That felt good to my hand and so must be
it. Before I went to sleep I resolved to put on the same
dress next time he had been drinking to see if his hand
was again attracted to it.

I would never wear that dress to the Sarajevo. The
bright colors would be too showy, making me all the more
plain. I would be afraid Luka would laugh at me, even
though I would like for his hand to be attracted to my bottom as Saša's was. Perhaps that had been an accident and

would not repeat itself. I would like to test it first on Saša, or even on Milorad. I could bring the dress in a bag, hiding it until Luka was absent. Then I would shower and put it on while still wet so that it would cling to me for Milorad to see.

I keep forgetting the shower has no water any more. Still, I could carry a bucket past Milorad to the shower and pour it over me there. Even though the waste is forbidden, I know he would follow me to watch and would never tell. However, it might not be a proper test as he is more shy than Luka and certainly more so than Saša. I'm sure, though, I could tell in his eyes whether or not his hand wanted to touch my bottom. If his eyes said yes, that would give me confidence and then I could try the dress with Luka. If Luka found out I let Milorad watch me, I would become even less desirable in his eyes but, in any case, I could pretend it was an accident and then he would blame Milorad.

Milorad is rather small for thirteen and so is often left behind when the others are out scavenging or fighting the Centrals. He's sensitive and quiet and when he's grown up, he says, he's going to be a poet, though as yet he certainly has nothing poetical to say. At least I haven't heard it. If he's written anything, he's hidden it away.

He's shy, in any case. I know what that's like. Once, when we still had school—I was in the second form—I had to go right in the middle of class. I tried hard, really concentrating, to wait for recess. I knew I should raise my hand and tell Teacher I had to go, but I couldn't. I wished at that time I was in the back near a corner, but my chair was almost in the middle of the room for all to see. You can see why I was unable to raise my hand. I wanted so to stick my arm up resolutely, straight and tall, and say loudly, "Please, may I be excused?" but part of me was afraid this would only bring laughter, which is death to shyness, so I did nothing at all except tighten myself up in a ball. Everything was devoted to holding my water, so I didn't even hear the teacher ask me a question. I must have looked like a zombie when the others stared at me. Later they would say, "Poor dumb Alma, gone away day-dreaming again!" Then I could hear everything as I felt my bladder release, and then the wet feel of shame running down my leg.

A puddle appeared on the floor that could not be explained away. Looking serious, I tried to put it off to a leaky roof, forgetting there had been no rain, so that my effort only brought the laughter I dreaded so much.

I was more glad that day for recess than ever before. Teacher was understanding, almost consoling in her quietness. She went with me to the cloakroom. There she had me remove my panties. I felt smaller and smaller, then open and vulnerable, as they descended my legs to the floor. I watched, hurt-eyed, as she rinsed them in the sink, then lay them over the radiator to dry. Then she gave me a pat on the head that said, "Poor dumb Alma," and left me to myself while they were drying. I spent the time looking at the coats and from them trying to imagine what the others' homes and families were like. I'm incredibly curious by nature.

I was right in the middle of this game, imagining my friend Dijana's mother as a big, beefy sort, her father as a butcher, when the bell ending recess rang and the happy, laughing sounds of returning students filled the other room. Though my panties were still wet to the touch, I grabbed them and, hastily pulling up my dress to speed things up, I almost had them on when I raised my eyes to find Luka staring intensely down at me. I was completely open to him, like I had to pee again, but different. His eyes inspected me, and I could tell I made him happy.

It's then I fell in love with him. Then I did something a shy Alma would never do. My eyes looked steadfastly at his and my lips teased him with a little smile as my fingers hesitated around the fringe of my panties. Then, casually, I pulled them up the rest of the way and dropped my dress.

It's the only time I've seen him at a loss. Stumbling on the words, "I've left my papers in my coat, you see," he brushed past me, and I could smell and feel the excitement of him in the closeness of the room. I'll never forget that. The power I had!

Later, in the classroom, I pretended to listen to Teacher, but actually was trying to conjure up the same feeling again as when his eyes were on me. I had a sudden impulse to open my legs slightly, but that's not nice, so I didn't. Only my knees quivered a little at the effort to keep them together. I regret even now that I wasn't brave enough to open them. Perhaps then Luka would have fallen in love with me instead of with the Princess Sandra.

So you can see I know what it's like, Milorad's being shy. I make up for it by daydreaming quite a lot, imagining myself in all sorts of roles. Sometimes I even think of the Sarajevo and our life here as a dream. We are so different from one another, but Luka holds us together. When we come here we leave our past lives behind, so I can forget to be shy.

I've forgotten now, as I lie here on Luka's mattress and pretend that he will find me. Yet all the while I know that when I hear them downstairs making a racket, proudly returning, I'll quickly but sadly pull my dress back down and leave Luka's room behind once again. I always hope that he'll catch the scent of me on his mattress and that it will set him to wondering if I was really here or not. Perhaps the smell of me here would make him want me here. I dream that he would be aroused, and jumping up, would come for me, not saying anything when he found me but simply taking me in his arms and carrying me back to be displayed on his bed. Then, looking him straight in the eyes, I would raise my dress again.

In my dream he rushes to me so eagerly that I lose sight of him, only feeling the heat of him flowing rapidly into my waiting body. If it were not a dream but real, it would be like the cloakroom, and he would no longer desire the Princess Sandra or Maud.

HOTEL

Sometimes when I'm having this dream I pinch the soft insides of my thighs till red marks appear, as though they were blushing for the want of him.

Luka's not a virgin, I know. He's fifteen, but already looks older and harder.

The first night I stayed in the Sarajevo there was a storm, and I was alone and afraid in my room, so I went quietly to Jasmina's room, knowing she would not tell. Only from outside her door I heard noises like groaning and, thinking she might be hurt or afraid, I opened the door a crack without any sound and found her and Luka right in the middle of it. I was not stunned because of Mother and Saša, but my eyes could only focus on the smooth whiteness of his straining and the hanging uselessness of her legs.

The next day I looked carefully at Jasmina's eyes, hoping they would tell me something of it. But they were quiet, and I was afraid to ask. Instead, as she talked to me about what school would be like when it started up again, I looked away from her eyes and out a window. So that finally Jasmina, laughing, snapped her fingers with, "Wake up, Alma. Daydreaming again?"

Even though I smiled at her my attention was elsewhere, and for a long time after, I was in the room with Luka.

I had never been envious of Jasmina before—she being my best friend—but suddenly I was. I was glad she didn't come every day, but only when she could find an excuse to break away from her family. When I saw her walk or run, the slightest shake of her breasts or hips took on a new significance that left me feeling empty and unwanted. I tried to bury myself in the pages of my book with Holden, but it no longer held my interest, and I could only think of Luka in the room with her.

Once, when I couldn't stand picturing them together any more, I wandered away from the Sarajevo alone, even though I could hear shelling quite close in the district. When you become used to it, the sound loses some of its terror. It's familiar, though it has a chameleon-like quality, being able to disguise itself, that makes it seem almost harmless.

I went down a narrow, stoned side street, then veered off abruptly to the left. I passed a mosque that was untouched and whose walls were an innocent shade of pink. Then I turned another corner and there was the Hotel Bristol fronting me, only not as it used to be. Formerly, with Mother, and then with Mother and Saša, we'd take a tram from the Boščaršija, peering out at the rose gardens along the way. Then we'd arrive, happy and laughing, for music and the dancing of the Kolo in a large circle in front of the hotel. It was a celebration of ourselves, and we all came in the spring and the fall, April and October.

But there was no longer music, only the screaming of angry rockets, and the only red was not of roses but from the fires exploding from the windows of the hotel, like a jack-o-lantern with candles inside that flared up angrily. Then I heard the screams and saw stick figures frantically rushing out with flames attached to their backs. It took me a moment to recognize and accept them as human, as though they were not connected to myself.

One old woman in particular I recall. Her hair was on fire and she had on a long shawl jacket that burned brightly as she ran screaming down the street. Watching her, I remembered the inscription on a stécci in the National Museum:

Here lies Orislav Kopijević.
I beseech you touch me not.
You will be as I am,
but I cannot be as you are.

In a moment the sound of fire trucks drowned out the screaming, and I felt out of place, a voyeur, because I was not burning. The others were made real by the flames growing from them, and I existed merely as a spectator.

What really gave me the shakes, however, and brought it all home to me was when some firemen carried out a young boy on a stretcher. He had not been burned but his legs were twisted at a grotesque angle, with a sharp white bone sticking out of one. Lying there, he seemed like a dwarf, stunted in his growth.

When I saw his eyes I was afraid, and sick too. I sat heavily on the curb and closed my eyes tightly, but I still saw his. They were flat and staring and horrible to see. I kept shaking my head to rid myself of them, but could not.

There was a touch on my arm that made me tremble all over but, opening my eyes, it was not the boy but a fireman. He was American, I think, because he spoke English funny. But I did not have much time to hear him as I tore myself away and ran from the horror of the boy's eyes back down the narrow streets the way I'd come, not stopping till I caught sight of the Sarajevo and entered it as I would a friend's confidence.

I didn't sleep that night. I wanted so to go to Luka's room and crawl into the safety of his arms to forget, but I was afraid he'd only make fun of me, calling me a frightened little girl. So I remained alone in the dark of my room, shaking uncontrollably and trying vainly to count the savage beats of my heart to slow it down.

The next morning I was still shaking, and what I really wanted, what my stomach craved, was a large piece of baklava, then some ručak, the warmth of the plum brandy washing down the sweet nut taste of the pastry. All we had, however, were some cold potatoes Ilija had found somewhere. We'd cooked them over an open fire in the courtyard the day before, singing and making a party of it. Even cold, the potato gave my mouth something to do, filling my belly and calming the rest of me.

I have only been that scared once before. It was before Saša and the war. Mother was to take me to the Church of Saint Archangela Michala to drink the holy fluid on his feast day.

It's said they take his hand from the reliquary and dip it in water that then becomes holy and has the power of healing the sick. They fill vials with it for us to drink. The night before, I imagined all sorts of things, then woke in a sweat. I'd been dreaming the hand was covering my face,

HOTEL

strangling me, until I was forced to kiss it and prostrate myself before it. Only then would it go away.

Actually, however, when we got our turn in line it was nothing at all. Mother drank first; then I raised the vial to my lips and was surprised to find the water merely had a faint sweet taste, nothing like what I had imagined, rather pleasant in fact. All the rest of the day I sat in front of a mirror and waited for a pimple to go away, but it never did. It's then, I think, I began to lose faith. But maybe the water only works for big cures and I was asking for something outside its province.

Sometimes I'm not sure of anything. Religion, I mean. Mother and I are Orthodox, but Milorad is a Muslim, and Ilija is a Jew. Luka is a gypsy and so nothing at all. He has no time for it, he says. He says we are all "cosmopolitans" because we are mixed together and married in the Sarajevo. There are times when I've felt I must have some gypsy blood because I've never really felt at home anywhere. But when I asked Mother, she was only annoyed and said to be quiet and not to ask silly questions.

When we used to go to church, the Pop was very sure of himself, surrounded by ceremony, confirming it all. But at midday when the muezzin climbs the minaret of the mosque and sings the ezan, "God is great and there is but one god, Allah," he seems just as sure.

The Husref Beg is the only mosque in Sarajevo where they still sing out ezan. The rest use loudspeakers.

I saw his turbe once. It was on the way home from the Boščaršija with Mother. The epitaph said, "Husref Beg

18

was overtaken by darkness in a state which was not sleep." That's how I felt the night I shook alone in my room, too frightened to dream of the boy with the empty eyes and the broken, twisted legs.

I don't know why I'm thinking of all these things now. I guess because I'd like to keep a clear picture in my mind of the way things were before the war so that, when it's over, I can go back to them straight away, humming and daydreaming again as though nothing had happened.

I can do that with Jasmina now. Her father had connections and they got a pass to Split, on the coast, that's been unaffected by the war. They left only last night. Jasmina came to the hotel one last time and, as she would no longer be a rival, I forgave her her night with Luka. There was nothing in my eyes as we hugged but a friendly good-bye.

Only I know I could never forget Luka and the Sarajevo. If the war were suddenly over and there was only Mother and Saša in the little flat, I know I would miss my life here, and my love for Luka would leave an emptiness in my heart. I never loved before.

If the sudden end of the war took Luka away from me, I would not be ready for that at all; and I know the aloneness, without love, with Mother and Saša in the flat, would be more threatening than the ring of soldiers with their guns and rockets on the hills above Sarajevo.

Not all the soldiers are bad or scary. There's Radman, who's different. He's French, but here he's what you call U.N. He's Jewish, like Ilija. I know because he wears a Star of David on a silver chain around his neck. Sometimes I look at the shining points of the star and imagine myself like that, bright and beautiful.

We're friends, he says, and I'm glad. I remember the day we met, in the fall. It was a Sunday. There was no shelling that day. The sun was out, smiling, and I was happy to walk down the Maršala Tita. Radman was seated outside a bife with friends, smiling too. Then they rose to leave and he was alone like me. He was drinking beer, which is expensive and hard to get, and eating ražnzici. The hot, satisfying fragrance of the skewered pork made me forget everything and sit right down at his table. Our eyes were staring at each other before I realized what I'd done. Part of me wanted to leave, but part of me wanted to stay also. He tried French first; then, when we discovered we had English in common, I was off in a burst, talking nonstop, as though we had known each other forever. I liked his smile, the friendliness of his teeth, and the way his hair blew about in the light fall breeze.

I guess he saw me staring at his plate because, still smiling, he pushed it toward me. But out of politeness I shook my head quickly. He asked what would I like and I burst out with, "sladoled! and cockta!" not thinking my wish would be satisfied, even wondering why I had dared to say it out loud. He smiled again, and before I could think to take it back, there appeared magically before me a dish of vanilla ice cream and a glass of cola. I can't tell you how my stomach thanked him for that, even as I watched, embarrassed, at the pile of dinars he counted out to pay for my extravagance. He must have noticed because he smiled again and patted my hand, putting the spoon, which I had hastily dropped, back in it. I returned his smile and began eating in earnest, not stopping to think to be shy until I had finished the ice cream and was washing it down with the cola. Then my eyes caught his over the glass and I lowered mine, embarrassed again. But when I looked into his eyes once more I knew that this was someone I didn't have to be shy with, so I promptly forgot and we became friends.

Radman is in love with Jan. I know because I've seen them kiss. It was once when they spotted me, alone and with nothing to do, in front of the Sarajevo. They took me with them down the street to the Café-Bar Lisac, which was then still open, but only for coffee mostly, and then only when it was available. Some things are smuggled in through the mountains and you can get them if you have money, as Jan and Radman have. She writes stories about us for some newspaper, I don't know which, and sometimes she leaves Sarajevo. Then Radman is sad and loses his smile, but when she returns again he is happy and his smile returns with her.

Before the war there was always a crowd of young people at the Lisac, laughing and listening to jazz and rock-and-roll, but on that day with Jan and Radman there was only a small radio blaring from the window of some flat above. To escape the heat of the sun on the open street

HOTEL

we moved to the small, enclosed courtyard behind the café, which was sheltered by vines and trees. It was safe and comfortable there, even when Jan and Radman left me sitting with my cola to walk among the trees. They were out of sight, but I heard their laughter. I followed them. Their laughter drew me. The vines brushed against my face, perfuming me. When at last I pulled back a vine to see Jan's and Radman's faces happily kissing one another, that's how I imagined a kiss to be—the soft perfume of a vine drawn softly across the lips.

I don't know much about kissing, mind you. There was only the time of Saša's wet, drunken kiss that was so sudden I scarcely remember the feel of it. But after watching Jan and Radman, I wanted to learn more about it so that one day I could offer my lips to Luka, making him want them. Perhaps it was Jan's red lipstick that made Radman want her lips.

I wish I could practice before I offer my lips to Luka, but I wouldn't know who to practice with. Radman would be perfect but he belongs to Jan, and I think I should ask her permission first. If she says yes, we could go back to the courtyard and I could learn all about kissing in private, and then I would be ready for Luka.

I'm afraid to imagine what our first kiss would be like. His lips would not be soft, but hard. Not hard, really, but strong. And their strength would conquer my softness and make me open to him. I've seen Jan and Radman exchange tongues when they kiss, so perhaps Luka would want that too, and, if so, I would be ready for him. I'm not sure exactly how it's done, but I would follow his lead. If only he wanted me!

When Jan and Radman are together you can feel the love between them, like the heat from oven-fresh pastry rising to your face. That's the way I want it to be with Luka and myself. When he comes home to the Sarajevo I would be waiting for him and he would want to tell me of his adventures. I would be the ears for his deeds, accepting and approving.

I try not to think of him too much because then the shyness rises up in me, and then when I see him I won't know what to say and he'll only think, "Poor dumb Alma!" and pass me by without a thought. I don't have his stories to tell or his bravery to boast of, but if he knew what my heart was like, that it was open to him and longed for him, that in my heart I'm not shy or plain but brave and beautiful, then I know he would love me as I love him.

It's beginning to get dark out, early because of the season. I want suddenly to roll over, kick my feet up, and spy on the passersby in the street below. I could make up stories about them and that would distract me for a while, taking me out of myself. If I were a boy I would like to be a writer when I'm grown. I guess a girl could be a writer too, like Jan, but unless she was just writing the news I really don't know what she would have to say that would be interesting. All I could tell about would be Mother and Saša, or Luka and things I've seen, and I don't know if anyone would want to hear about that.

I hear voices, happy and yelling in the street below. It's

HOTEL

Luka and the others. The thought of him returning fills me with excitement, even though it means I must leave his room where I have been happy.

Once I thought, "What if Luka doesn't come back with the others?" but the sudden fear that idea provoked made me shut it down quickly, and I've never thought of it again. I *know* he will be here in a moment strutting and boasting in the lobby, happy to be the chief. Even though there is little to eat now, he will still proudly display whatever it is they've managed to scavenge, and I will be happy for him. It's his way of being himself, as mine was when I hesitated in pulling up my panties in the cloakroom.

Once he brought me a scarf, sun-colored. He offered it to me off-handedly and I grabbed at it, not even thinking to refuse. I could tell his eyes were pleased with the quickness of my acceptance. He would be pleased too, I know, if he knew that later I put its silky softness against the throbbing growing of my breasts and drifted off to sleep imagining it as his hand there.

I get up reluctantly to go, as I hear their voices louder outside in the street. I pull down my dress, smoothing it, and sadly leave his bed, a hard mattress on the floor.

But before I leave the room I go to the window, careful, however, that none of them see me. I'm curious what all the yelling's about. The rain has stopped, but still there's no sun.

It's only Mira next door they're tormenting with their taunts, even throwing rocks against her "house." She

24

lives in an abandoned kiosk on the sidewalk near the hotel. It's not as ludicrous as it seems. It serves to keep the
rain off her quite well and, in any case, she says it's all she
deserves. She broke out one side with a board one day and
climbed in, making herself at home.

She's from the countryside around Mostar and somehow made her way here just after the siege began. She's
never talked of what happened to her there, but I've
heard grownups in the street whisper and point to her.
They say she was raped repeatedly until pregnant, that
she escaped and aborted it herself, without help. Once
they were making fun of her and two men laughed and
made as if one was a horse and the other riding it. At that
point I hated them for their cruelty. They also say she's
crazy, but I don't believe it, only that her eyes have seen
too much.

I would like to be kind to her in some way, but I don't
know how. Once I had my chance but blew it. I was outside playing hopscotch as she was returning home. For
some reason she became interested in my game, watching
me intently, and making little bird-like sounds that
frightened me. She came near, gesturing to her house
with one hand and putting the other on my arm. I think
she wanted me to visit her there, but the coldness of her
hand and the strangeness of her eyes made me balk, and,
pulling away, I ran quickly inside the hotel. When I
looked back through a crack in the door, she had disappeared inside the kiosk. Then I felt bad. Perhaps she had

wanted to tell me something or was proud of something she had found in the street and wanted to display it, as Luka finds happiness in doing.

I feel bad again now as I watch the Jevos pelting her house and calling after her. But they're men, or boys anyway, and what do they know after all? I know in my heart she'll never come out to face them. A woman would rather die inside than be made a mockery of.

I would like to fling open the window and shout at them to stop, or rush down the stairs into the street to berate them for their unfeeling cruelty. But I do not, for to question Luka's authority would only make me less in his eyes.

So I go sadly to the door of his room, hoping they will soon leave her in peace to her own remembered misery. Before I close the door I look back at the mattress, at the disturbed sheets and the impression my being there has left in them, and I hope that when Luka lies alone in the night he will find a comfort in the outline of me there beneath him.

THEY BURST THROUGH THE DOOR like young warriors: Luka first, then the rest, bright-faced, flushed, energetic. They're wet from the rain, and that makes them seem even more intense. Ilija and Nenad, the quiet one, wheel the bikes into the lobby. They are our treasure, and we would be lost without them. Their speed allows us to get away with swiping food and other necessities from the Centrals, as well as giving us a certain status over them.

Fighting the Centrals is everything in our lives, Luka says. It's a ritual that's been going on since just after the start of the war. It's understood no weapons are allowed except rocks, and they're mostly to make noise, I think. Luka says that it's better to take than to beg, and we all agree with him, except perhaps Milorad, who is sometimes afraid.

Once I caught Milorad crying under a stairwell. He didn't know I was there as I sat above him on the steps and listened to the sounds he made. Later I wondered at my lack of feeling, only allowing that I was curious. I don't remember crying, ever.

HOTEL

"We are home," Luka announces, raising high with both hands a bag of rice. His face is one big smile.

Dejan, his lieutenant, a big, sad-faced boy, but tough, drops a larger, heavier bag of flour, then pulls it to the center of the lobby, displaying it there for all to see. He is silent, but you can see the pride in his eyes.

A door opens above and the Princess Sandra quietly comes to the railing. I look away as Luka bounds up the stairs to her. To keep from thinking, I congratulate the others.

They chanced on a Red Cross truck, it seems, in a poor quarter near the Boščaršija. Ilija and his sister, Nihada, stood there still and silent and so forlorn that a worker felt sorry for them and pushed the bags off the truck with, "Take it home to your mama." As soon as the truck rounded a corner, all the rest of the Jevos rushed forward to give Ilija a joyful thump on the back.

I'm aware of Luka and Sandra on the landing above and can't help raising my eyes. She has a hand on the railing as he proudly comes to her, and just before his hand closes over hers, I rush forward to give Ilija a hug, smiling at him, even though inwardly I'm seething with jealousy. What a difference it would make to an Alma to be the one that Luka comes to!

Milorad comes out of hiding. He seems to be able to disappear at times into the depths of the hotel, where no one can find him.

Luka calls out, "See what you've missed out on!" I look up again in spite of myself to see him grinning, as usual.

SARAJEVO

Everything is fun and a great joke to Luka. He has an arm around Sandra and is holding a plastic bag of mixed pills aloft. My look scolds Ilija, who shrugs his shoulders. Later he would tell me no one knew where Luka got them. He'd only told them to wait; then he'd gone off alone, to come back smiling.

I don't like it, but can say nothing. He doesn't get drugs often, less now than before, but when he does he becomes moody and sullen, making me even more obscure to him.

Once I came upon him in the bathroom. At first it was so dark I couldn't see, so I proceeded to do my business, humming a little as I sat. I've always liked the cold feel of the tile. Then as my eyes became adjusted, he was suddenly there opposite me, not looking in my direction but turned to the side, totally unaware of my presence. I was startled and my legs quickly closed together. Then I could see he was out of it and I was only curious, wondering where he had gone to and what it was like. Was it anything like daydreaming?

He still didn't move, even when I'd finished, so I called his name softly. After a second he turned his face to me, but it was not the face of Luka, and I could tell in his eyes that I was not there for him.

A heavy sorrow for him pushed me like a blow, and I went to him and stood looking down at him. Then I knelt and put my arms around him, drawing his head to me. He gave no sign, but when I released him he seemed to want to cling a bit, and I felt like a mother with her

29

baby. For a few days after that, each time he saw me his eyes lingered, as though trying to recall something he'd forgotten.

He's never let any of us use the drugs, keeping them to himself. I don't know where he got started on them, if it was before the war or afterwards, in the Sarajevo. I don't think he knows what he takes or why, only that it takes him out of himself. I can understand that. Many times when I look in the mirror I'd like to go away from it all.

The Princess Sandra is smiling at Luka, proud that she exists for him. With a wave to us he turns to go off alone with his pills, but then he stops and offers Sandra his hand. This is significant, as it's never happened before, and I can't help feeling another tinge of jealousy.

Sandra takes Luka's hand, and they disappear from the landing. Ilija is surprised, but says nothing. He always follows Luka blindly. I think if Luka, smiling, rushed into a burning building, Ilija would rush to join him, also smiling.

With Luka gone we're at a loss, milling around in the lobby, boisterous but contained. Then Ilija's suddenly in front of me and, smiling, shoves a chocolate bar into my hands. "Come with us next time," he says.

Along with the flour and rice they've managed to scrape up some canned goods—quite a day's work—and they all rush off to the courtyard to make a feast over the fire.

I'm left alone with Milorad in a corner. He hasn't taken his eyes off the chocolate, and I can tell he expects me to

SARAJEVO

share. I sit on the stairs, peeling the wrapper, knowing he'll join me. So when he sits down silently beside me, I offer him a piece. Nihada, who's nine, comes to the bottom of the stairs and looks at us sadly. She has a crush on Milorad, but he pays her no mind.

Suddenly I feel like talking. "Why don't you go with the others?" I can tell by his squirming that my question bothers him, so I offer him another square of chocolate.

"I'm going to be a poet, you know, someday when I'm big." That's funny to hear him say with his mouth full.

"Why did you stare at me, that time in the shower?" I ask him. But then he starts squirming again.

"I have a knife. Want to see?" Happily, without waiting for approval, he pulls it from a pocket and opens it for me. It's small but sturdy, and I pull it across my finger to test its sharpness.

"Careful! You'll cut yourself!" The sound of his voice irritates me.

Too late. A thin strip of red, not painful though, appears magically on my fingertip. It's interesting to watch it spread, and I'm absorbed in that. Milorad takes my hand in his small one and squeezes the finger hard.

"It will bleed for a minute; then it will stop," he says with authority.

"You're hurting me!" I protest, but he continues to squeeze until he's satisfied; then he lets my hand drop.

Then, I don't know why, I lean over and kiss him on the cheek. It's softer than mine.

HOTEL

Immediately a deep blush spreads across his face. I reach to kiss him again and he's off like a laughing rocket.

"Milorad is a 'fraidy cat!" I call after him, rubbing it in, but his only response is more laughter as he runs after the others to the courtyard.

Outside it's already dark. They've got the fire going. It's safe. You can't see it from the front and, anyway, there's no shelling now.

If you've never seen rocket fire at night, it's a real show. Raining down from the hills, it's like falling stars or a fireworks show on Labor Day. No matter how much you're used to them, they always surprise you. There's only a quiet, whistling noise until they hit. Then if they're far away there's no fear; only if one hits close there's a rumbling that starts me shaking and I want to be held, but there's no one to ask without feeling small inside.

I dreamed once that Luka and I were in love. We were sitting and holding one another, each just content in the other's presence. There was one big burst high from a hill, and we watched it coming in the dark. Then there was just nothing, and I woke up.

They're all there around the fire, except for Luka and the Princess Sandra, of course, looking like one big family, or students in a classroom.

I used to miss school, believe it or not, when there was just Mother and Saša before I came to the Sarajevo, but now it's okay.

SARAJEVO

Father was never anything more than an absence. When Mother and I were alone in the flat we mostly stayed out of each other's way, moving silently through the rooms like two ghosts.

I never felt like a child. I don't remember playing like the other children. Then Saša came and played games with me and made me laugh. Luka doesn't make me laugh, and I can't say exactly why I love him. I only know that I do.

As I look into the fire, squatting next to it, I want so for Jan to be here. Not here next to the fire, but in Sarajevo. That way I could go visit her, or she would find me, and I would tell her of my love for Luka.

She could never come to the courtyard. It's off limits to adults, and we would fight to keep them out. Luka made that rule when he first carved his name on the tree. It's better that way, he says. We don't need any of them. We're entirely self-sufficient.

Sometimes I wonder what will happen to us when we grow up. Will we remain here together, or go our separate ways? I can't imagine myself as ever being any different than I am now, except my breasts will be larger.

I would like to talk to Jan now because Luka is gone away to the room with the Princess Sandra. I wonder if he took her with him because he's afraid when he goes away by himself, not knowing if he'll come back. He could never show fear in front of the Jevos. He would lose face. Being chief is all he cares for. It's like he's never known anything else. The war was made for him. It created us for him, pulling us out of our different lives and dropping us down *plop!* in the Sarajevo to be led by Luka.

Once he returned from a raid against the Centrals and I saw his eyes shining, as if he were doing drugs. I'm sure his eyes do not allow him to see an end to the war. I can't see him in a mechanic's overalls climbing from underneath a car, or behind the wheel of a truck. Once you've been a chief, all other occupations must seem meaningless, so for him the ending of the war could only mean defeat.

I never try to think of us together after the war. That's too far. Except for the shower, there's little that I miss.

Ilija is on one side of me, Milorad on the other, like a large baby hanging onto my presence. Neither of them has ever been with a girl, I'm sure, though Ilija likes to make up stories and boast.

They're saving the rice and flour, heating the potatoes again first.

Before the war, I watched Mother make kacamak in the hot little kitchen that always seemed too small, especially with Saša's mass in it. The ground maize was cooked in salt water, then eaten with milk and sugar or cream and cheese, with maize bread on the side. I was always filled when I finished.

Now, as with every meal, I take a mouthful of the hard potato and chew very carefully, closing my eyes as I do so.

This time it takes me back to a day I spent with Mother. We were at a kiosk near the orange station booth. I was

SARAJEVO

looking up at a billboard of Vučko, wishing I were as sly as he. We were on our way to have pizza, something I love, at the Dubrovnik Pizzeria, straight down from the Boščar-šija toward the Miljacka. It was spring and there were flowers, and music from radios in all the windows, and no sniper fire either, so we didn't have to run, but could take our time so we'd be properly hungry when we arrived . . .

"I'm worried about Luka." Dejan's voice sorrowfully brings me back to the courtyard and the fire, and I taste cold potato and not hot pizza.

"Luka can take care of himself." Ilija always takes up for him, and that makes me like him, even if he does lie about being with girls.

"They've been gone a long time." Dejan, the worrier.

Ilija smiles and winks at Dejan, then pokes me in the side with an elbow, making me bite my tongue. I'm furious, but I'm not certain if it's because of the pain or his insinuation. I don't try to get back at him because fighting among ourselves is forbidden. Luka says we're all any of us has, and we must save ourselves to fight the Centrals.

Making a real effort, I swallow my mouthful of potato. It's like I've been chewing forever. When I daydream, time loses itself for me.

I saw a film once in school called *Hiroshima Mon Amour*. It means Hiroshima My Love. Teacher explained the film, saying it was about time and memory, so I was very interested, though I didn't understand it all. It was plain to see that they wanted to be in love but were afraid to be. I don't know what made them afraid. I never exactly wanted to be in love, never thought of it rather, but once I was and knew it, I was never afraid.

Now I want Jan next to me at the fire more than ever, rather than Ilija. She'd understand. I went to see her once when she and the other writers had a group of rooms in a low building that was protected from the shelling by other, taller ones. From the train station you walk down Krančeviča, then you're there. There used to be a kebob place next door, and when I saw it in ruins its absence rumbled in my stomach. But that went away immediately as I ducked my head and ran across the street.

Jan saw me through a window and rushed out to pull me inside. She had on a flack jacket, but she'd forgotten her helmet. I started to remind her, but we were already inside and her arms were around me as she said, "How did you get here, child? You have no business about in the street." Her closeness made me go limp and lean against her. But I wondered what would happen if suddenly we couldn't bear things any longer and just broke down, falling like rag dolls in the middle of the street and crying. That thought scared me and I pushed it out of my mind.

Jan pushed me back to look at me, and she smiled and I forgot everything and was happy. A smile is like giving someone a surprise birthday card and really meaning it. She asked me again how I got there and I told her, "I just came. No one paid any notice to me."

"I only have a few minutes. I have to be at the airport. But come, we can chat." I felt an emptiness again as she took my hand and led me to her room.

SARAJEVO

Laughing, she sat me on her bed, and she sat before a mirror at a small desk she'd made into a make-up table. She started applying eye make-up, looking at herself in the mirror as she talked. I was fascinated. Mother never used make-up, considering it a waste of time. I asked her about it once and she only laughed, saying it was something a woman did for herself, not for a man and, anyway, she didn't see the expense and so took no stock in it.

But Jan was really enjoying herself, though she was beautiful without the make-up.

"Come here." She turned and held out her hand to me. "We'll make you beautiful before I go." She began applying make-up to my face. I don't remember the feel of her hands, but what I recall is the sound of her voice saying, "beautiful." Finally, she said, "finished," and turned me to the mirror. I was afraid to look. What I wanted more than anything was to be confronted with a Princess Alma staring back at me. I wanted to close my eyes, then open them to be beautiful, but I didn't because I was afraid she would think it was childish. So immediately, without any preparation, I looked. It was not what I'd expected. What my wide, tentative eyes saw was the old Alma with make-up. It did nothing but accentuate my plainness, outlining it. I tried to hide my disappointment, even attempting a smile, but behind it, deep inside, all hope for a beautiful Alma faded and drowned in tears I didn't show, but which were real nonetheless.

Jan was pleased with her work. Leaving me in front of the mirror, she went about the business of packing, just one small suitcase. She was happy until she took a brightly colored scarf from a drawer. Then her face changed and was sad, and she hesitated over putting it in the suitcase. I knew without her telling me that it was a gift from Radman.

Her shoulders shook a bit as she sat on the bed with her head lowered. She played with the scarf, feeling its softness. I heard her quiet crying. I caught a last look in the mirror and saw a made-up clown, not a happy one either. Then I went to Jan. My hand reached for hers and she took it. Her eyes brightened and she put the scarf in my hands. "Keep it for me," she said, wiping away her finished tears. Now she was happy. I knew she wanted it to remain here in Sarajevo, where Radman would remain while she was gone, as a symbol of their love.

I saw her off. She waved to me from the truck.

Afterwards, all the way home I fingered the silkiness of the scarf, glad that Radman loved her and had given it to her.

Before I reached the Sarajevo, I stopped at the Sebilj public fountain and washed the make-up off with my sleeve, so as not to be laughed at.

Ilija jumps up, startling me. In the dark, looking up at him, he seems big and old. For an instant I think of the soldier who raped me on the hillside of Zuc, and it's he standing above me. I remember that my eyes felt sad for him, as though they'd been separated from the rest of me.

SARAJEVO

I got the impression there was something in my look he feared.

But Ilija is not looking at me, but toward the double doors opening onto the courtyard. My eyes follow his to see Luka and Sandra framed there by the light from the fire. Across the fire from me with the dark behind them, they appear to be in the fire, being burned by it.

When Luka smiles and puts his arm around Sandra, I'm suddenly cold, and I want to be in the fire with them.

I WANT TO ASK LUKA right away to take me to the Town
Hall to see the dead lovers, but his eyes prevent me
from blurting it out. They're still glassy, and I don't think
he sees me. Sandra's are the same as his, and I'm jealous
again.

Ilija pushes a cup of turska kava into Luka's hands,
then sets in front of him a plate of režička pršuta they've
saved out for him. I don't mind. I don't like it anyway. The
smoked beef is too hard to chew.

Luka slowly drinks the coffee but ignores the food.
Sandra leans on him and clutches his arm with her tiny
hand. They haven't let her see any of the war or the shelling. Sometimes I envy her that and sometimes I don't.
There are things I wish I hadn't seen, but at the same
time I feel older and wiser. Later, when I have children, I
can tell them that I was in Sarajevo during the siege, saying it proudly for them to marvel at.

I do not feel older and wiser because of the soldier taking me on Zuc. Now I do not have that to offer Luka. No
one knows, so there's none of the laughter and insults like
those flung at Mira, but I know.

If Sandra had been on Zuc for him to take that day,

SARAJEVO

I wonder if she would have been too terrified to scream. I remained silent not out of fear, but because screaming would only have drawn attention to my violation. I was lucky not to become pregnant with his baby, but if I had, I would have given birth to it proudly, even if it meant going away to hide. It would have been a little bit of Alma, and I would have held it and made faces at it to make it happy.

I had a doll once. Mother got it for me. It was a Raggedy Ann. She looked like me with her big eyes, but her hair was red. After Father left, we moved to a smaller flat. Then the doll disappeared and was lost, Mother said.

Sandra looks fragile and vulnerable as her head drops onto Luka's shoulder.

They've never even let her see Mira. The hotel and the courtyard are her whole world. For her it's as if the war didn't exist, except for the noise of the rockets.

We don't know anything of her life before she came to us. One day she was just sitting on the steps with those same inexpressive eyes, waiting for us to take her in. Everything about her seems soft, as though she could form herself into any shape she wanted. Luka recognized her worth right away and made her one of us.

Luka's becoming himself again. Shaking his head, he downs the coffee in one swallow, then starts in hungrily on the food.

No one holds Luka's drugs against him. It's accepted. I don't like it, but I don't question it. Though when he's on them it seems as if he's dead, and that upsets me.

HOTEL

Once in the middle of winter I was out with Ilija trying to find wood. The snow suddenly became heavy and we were lost in it. At first the soft white sting of the flakes was exhilarating, as though we were in a fairy land, bright and pure, hiding us and protecting us. Then I heard noises that became sobs as we made our way through the blinding snow. Without warning we came on an old woman on her knees, crying and tearing at a make-shift wooden cross with her fingernails.

What I immediately thought was, "This is dead." Ilija just looked at her blankly, immune to her suffering. Though I could tell he wanted the wood badly, he reluctantly turned away, pulling me by the arm. I hesitated, wanting to do something for her. He pulled harder and I went with him, glad that his strength and decision freed me from the need to help her.

After a few yards we could no longer hear her sobs, and I don't know if she died there in the snow or if, when she finished grieving, she got up and went away. I never saw her face; she had a scarf wound tightly about her head.

A little farther on we came upon more crosses, maybe ten of them. Ilija was delighted with our luck, jumping from one to the other knocking them over, then filling both our arms.

"Luka will be pleased!" he yelled at me through the snow, and the thought of Luka's approval made me happy in what we were doing. I kicked over the last cross myself and was sorry there were not more for us to bring to Luka.

SARAJEVO

On the way home, even though my arms got tired carrying the crosses, I was bolstered by the thought that burning them would help to warm Luka, and I thought, "Warm is alive." Then I wished I could go back and find the cross of the old woman, which could do her no good, and carry it, too, to Luka to keep him alive.

Luka is certainly alive now, laughing and joking with the others. Sandra hasn't completely recovered. She's still and vacant, her eyes trying to find recognition wherever they turn. Luka waves his hand in front of her and everyone laughs. She certainly makes a funny picture.

When Sandra finally comes around, everyone is happy over her triumph and Luka is content to let her be the center of attention for the moment. Ilija mashes a potato to make it soft for her, then serves it to her with rice cakes.

Milorad nuzzles up to me near the fire, and I let him. His mother was killed by a sniper early in the siege. Perhaps now his body remembers, but not his mind.

Dejan pulls out a harmonica that he found in a trash pile. He taught himself to play. He must be naturally sad, because that's the only sound that comes out when he blows on it.

"Not now, Dejan. We don't need your funeral music tonight." Luka stops his playing, but he is smiling, not mean.

Luka's smile and the fuss they're making over Sandra make me feel alone.

HOTEL

I wonder if Mother and Saša are happy together there in the little flat. I've never really thought of Mother as having the quality of either happy or unhappy, just acceptance.

This is the longest I've been gone from the flat, almost two weeks. I didn't tell Mother about Luka and the Sarajevo. She quite simply accepted my absences as she accepts everything else.

At least I know they're not hungry. Saša, I think, has some sort of connections with the black market. He's always able to get food and necessary items, in any case. I think it's what kept him out of the army. I picture him again standing in the kitchen of the flat, lighting a cigar and puffing on it, saying, "A man must know how to survive," his eyes gleaming.

Some days when there's little or no shelling I wander down the narrow streets to the Boščaršija to watch the well-fed people there. They're eating, laughing, and talking just as if there were no war. And while I'm fascinated by their indifference, I feel a faint disgust for them. Jan calls them "hangers-on" and "interlopers." That wasn't in my book about Holden, but by the sneering mockery of her voice I know it wasn't meant to be nice.

I've never really understood the war. It just *was* one day, without any grown-up explanation for it, and so also to be accepted.

Acceptance was the time we went in a group to Kosevo Hospital to see Adnan. He'd lost both legs to a grenade attack.

SARAJEVO

We all pushed our way into the lobby, letting Luka do the talking.

"We want to see our friend, Adnan. He's one of us."

"Impossible; there's too many of you. It won't be allowed."

Luka took the refusal of the nurse in stride, sitting down in the middle of the floor and crossing his arms. We all followed his example. In a minute the nurse came back and started up again.

"You'll have to leave. You're in the way."

"We want to see our friend." Luka was like a rock, face determined, chin jutted out, arms still crossed. I wanted to be like him.

"Alright. But only three of you, not the whole lot. And only for a minute."

I was thrilled when the nurse pointed to Ilija and myself because we were seated on either side of Luka.

The stairs were dark as we climbed them behind the nurse. I didn't know Adnan, only that he'd been wounded before I came to the Sarajevo.

Luka carried a small package wrapped in plain brown paper to give to him.

At the top of the stairs Ilija suddenly turned to me and said, "Don't stare at his legs. Make believe there's nothing wrong."

Outside the ward the nurse said curtly, "You can't stay long," and you could tell we were merely a nuisance to her.

Inside, the atmosphere was dim and depressing. I heard the patients before I saw them. There was a stifled groan as we passed the foot of a bed, telling me of its occupant. I had never thought of pain as having a sound before; it scared me a little.

When we arrived at Adnan's bed I found myself staring at the railing as Luka called out to him, "We're here, comrade!" The cheerfulness of his voice made it okay to look, and I was relieved to see Adnan covered by a sheet from the waist down. He was pale and thin and had beads of sweat on his forehead that made me a little nauseous.

Luka and Ilija were bouncing on his bed as Adnan gleefully ripped the paper off a toy gun. They must have pinched it from Yosef's store somehow.

Adnan brought the gun to his shoulder with "*Pow! Pow!*" not even bothering to aim.

"I kill you," he said to no one in particular, though he seemed proud of his marksmanship. Ilija slapped him on the back. Luka took the little face in his hands and said, "We do not forget our friend."

Adnan began pelting Luka and Ilija with questions: What was the Sarajevo like now? Had the Centrals been defeated?

His legs were forgotten as I sat on the bed and pretended to be interested in his new gun.

"I'm going to kill Vladan when I return home," Adnan said. "I will make an ambush for him. Then our war with them will be over."

Luka and Ilija cheered him on and their bouncing and yelling made my stomach uneasy. The room seemed to grow smaller, and now my forehead had beads of sweat also. The more Adnan carried on, smiling and shooting the gun —*pow!*—over and over, the more uncomfortable I was sitting where his legs should have been.

I had heard the nurse say that gangrene had set in, that they were powerless to prevent it. Suddenly I knew he would die here, and I began sweating even more. Luka must have noticed it because he said as he looked at me, "Wait outside for us." I was grateful for his words and got up quickly, mumbling a good-bye to Adnan.

I heard him call out, "See you again!" but that only hurried me along, though it took forever to pass the beds that each contained small bundles of pain.

I was careful not to look until at the last bed I had to. There was a young girl, five or six, lying there eyes open, dried blood on her lips, with an arm outstretched toward a doll just out of her reach. I wanted to reach the doll to her to comfort her, but couldn't make myself do it. Her eyes remained the same as I darted out the door to the safety of the hall.

The door closed behind me and I could no longer hear their cries, but only the thumping fear of my heart as my useless fingers pressed into the hardness of the wall.

Luka and Ilija came out. I shut my eyes when the door opened, like that could keep sound out, then opened them when the door closed.

Ilija said excitedly, "We'll see him again soon!" but Luka looked at me with more truth than Ilija's words.

HOTEL

Even with Dejan's music and Milorad's snuggling close, loneliness grabs me by the throat and makes me shout frantically to Luka, "Please, can you take me to see the lovers?" I almost added "dead," but didn't.

Luka doesn't answer right away, but his look asks me why.

I can't make an answer. How can I tell him that I feel she's like a lost sister? I know that, even dead, they need our presence to validate their love, an acceptance denied them in life.

Luka takes pleasure in my discomfort. Finally he answers flatly, "They don't concern us."

He turns away, but when he touches Sandra's arm I know it's she he'll take instead.

Suddenly I am filled with a great anger at life. I care nothing for the fire, or the food, or their company, but only want to lose myself somewhere.

I get up as quietly as possible so as not to attract notice, and go inside.

There, as soon as I'm sure I'm alone, I begin running. I'm not afraid of stumbling; I know every piece of furniture, even in the dark. I don't stop until I've closed the door to my room behind me and thrown myself on the bed in a tight little ball.

Later I awake to the sounds of shelling far off. Milorad is beside me with his arm around me. I hear him crying, just stifled sobs against my back. They bring me comfort, as I have none of my own.

I WAKE EARLY TO FIND myself alone. I dress hurriedly
without even pausing to eat. I'm not hungry anyhow;
I've never been a big eater. Even with Mother and Saša,
sometimes I would just sit and stare at my plate.

I leave the hotel quietly, like a thief escaping. I think
I've got away clean, but as I reach the street the big, heavy
front doors open with a creak, and Milorad is there with
his sleepy, questioning face.

"Where are you going?" His plaintiff whisper from the
stairs betrays his fear of being left behind.

"Go back to sleep. It's not for you." My low voice is
strange in the stillness, like I'm breathing out little clouds
that hang in the air.

Milorad stands there big-eyed, his hand on the iron
rail, as though the railing holds him back. Nihada appears at the door behind him.

Walking away, I still feel his eyes on me, so I call to him
playfully, "Go back, little nuisance, with your girlfriend."
The doors creak again and then I'm free.

The light is grey, like a charcoal drawing, and I like the
early chill. It's like waking up to see a friend's face, or the
first strong taste of turska kava.

HOTEL

I've always liked to walk the streets alone. There's always so much to see. I can make a story out of almost anything. If a grocer comes out to open his shop and display his wares, I think about that, wondering what he hopes for and expects from the day. If there is a frown or some sadness on his face, I try to imagine what secret sorrow lies behind it.

There's no one about as yet. I planned it that way. I'm going to the Town Hall to see the lovers to pay silent tribute to them.

The old Town Hall is on the Vojvode Stepe near the river. It's a long walk and I'll be tired when I get there. I'll want to rest. There's a curved walk and, just in the middle under some trees, a favorite bench of mine. Maybe I'll be hungry, but I won't think about my stomach for the tiredness in my legs and the anticipation of seeing the lovers.

The only danger will be when I pass the Morića Han. It's very old, a converted caravanserai. It's right on the way, at Saraši 77 in the heart of the Boščaršija. I can't avoid it without going out of my way. They'll already be preparing the morning's coffee and rolls, and the smells might distract me, causing me to linger. But I'll steel myself to that so I'll look neither right nor left. I want nothing to frustrate my desire to be first in line when the doors of the Town Hall open to allow the curious in.

It's strange all the furor it's aroused. Many others have died. You get used to it. Maybe that's why they died in

50

SARAJEVO

each other's arms while trying to escape—to remind us not to get used to it.

I'm glad that they've finished their suffering. It's over for them. Before, they were just suffering. Now they're to be congratulated. Even lying dead, exposed in the field near the river, they were dead suffering. That is for dogs, not for people. Not for dogs even. Death is a completion and should be a private affair. Their death was unique to them, just as their love was, as mine for Luka is.

I'm not alone in the street anymore. Coming toward me, there's an old man peddling a bicycle. I can't see his face until he's quite close. I want him to raise a hand and call out to me, but he doesn't look up, so I remain unknown to him.

There are more people in the streets when I come to the Boščaršija; and the fresh, strong smell of coffee surrounding me. I'm tempted to sit down in front of a café and abandon myself to the sights and smells, but I shake my head and hurry on.

Walking faster, I round a corner and there's the Miljacka below me. There's a mist coming off it, like the steam from the coffee, making me comfortable inside.

I hurry down the hill and then I'm on the Vojvode Stepe. It's one of my favorite streets, so I don't hurry so much now, but enjoy it. It's very wide, with an island of trees. When it's warm, there are flowers. I'm completely at ease, knowing my walk is a success. I'll see the lovers and be gone before Luka and Sandra even arrive.

HOTEL

My feet are not tired, but happy, when I reach the crescent walk and the bench. I can see the still-closed doors of the Town Hall. There's no one before me.

I want to see the lovers' faces to know what kind of beauty would attract the arms of a man around you in death, to know what sort of man would want to die with you like that. I wonder if they had time to whisper their love before it was over.

I'm staring at the doors so hard, as though that will magically make them open, that I'm startled to find someone near me. He's a young boy, slightly older than myself, with dark hair and deep eyes.

His gaze throws me a little, and before I can stop him he turns and heads for the doors, *my* doors.

Defeated, I can only follow.

Inside, the dark is broken only by the winking of candles here and there. For a moment it's as if I'd imagined him, but when my eyes get used to the light, he's there alongside the coffins. He has a serious look about him. I'm not ready to make up stories about him, just curious who he is and what brought him here to take my place as first in line.

"They're asleep," he says, as though it's a fact and they had indeed defeated death just by closing their eyes in its face.

"Yes, they're happy now." I reply frankly what I feel. I wouldn't have said it in the presence of Luka. I would have made up something that I thought would please him.

SARAJEVO

He steps aside as though acknowledging me, allowing me a closer look, and I like that.

The lovers' coffins are set on sawhorses. They're a few feet apart so you can walk between them. I suppose it allows more people to see them at once, but it's strange that they should be separated. How constricting their boxes must be after the open field of their death.

"They should be together." The boy must have known what I was thinking, and I'm glad he understands.

We're alone with the lovers, almost. In the candlelight I'm only vaguely conscious of the little withered old man who opened the doors. He's half hidden by the shadows, but I can make out his face in the light. Then there's the sound of the doors and his face is gone to attend to it.

The boy says, "Quickly." He's at the head of the woman's coffin and I'm at the foot. We lift it on its horses and set it next to the other, where it rightfully belongs.

When the caretaker's face returns to its place in the light, we're as before. Only now we're happy for the lovers, and happy for ourselves that we managed so well.

We're no longer alone with them, however. Other curious faces intrude, pushing their way in. It's not the same as before, so moving as one, my helper and I turn to leave.

At the door, suddenly afraid for the lovers, I jerk my head around. But there's the boy in my face and all I can say is, "I don't know your name."

He's so close I can smell all the different odors that make him up—his hair and his skin and the material of

HOTEL

his jacket and the perfume from the burning candles. So I feel like I already know him, so when he answers, "Omar," I'm not surprised at all.

On tiptoes, I look over his shoulder as we go out the doors, and the last thing I see is the candlelight flickering off the lovers' faces, like haloes. And that's the image I'll always have of them.

THE SQUARE IS SILENT. There's no one about except a cat I don't recognize. It looks at me flatly, then moves away.

It's not really a square, only a concrete courtyard in front of the building. I've always called it that to lend my building some dignity. Now, however, I'm sorry for it. It's deserted, and there're big, gaping holes here and there, like an old person vainly smiling with only half their teeth. The building must feel as I did when the soldier finished with me on Zuc.

After I left Omar and the sanctuary of the lovers, I felt the need to return to Mother and the little flat. The lovers' coffins reminded me of its narrowness.

When I went away, the building was as always. Maria played her radio too loudly upstairs, perhaps in an effort to escape her solitude, and everything was normal. I wasn't close to Mother and Saša, but their presence and their silences were there, reassuring.

If you walked into a room where Mother was, it was a while before you knew that the room contained her. Sometimes I think that the noises a person makes are the lasting impression you have of them. Saša was all noise

HOTEL

and motion—drunken noise, it's true, but at least not that silent acceptance Mother bequeathed me.

Luka's noise is haughty and commanding, but you can't hold that against him: he's the chief. I'm probably the only one who understands there's an element of bluster behind his noise, but I never let on, only smiling inwardly.

Staring at the ruins of my building, I think of Omar in the sanctuary and wonder what noises he would make to define himself. There he was only quiet, like whispers in the night. That's how I thought of us: two children whispering stories at bedtime, just after the lights have been turned off. It's partly to defeat the turning out of the lights, proving how big we are, but really it's the natural language we use to communicate. During the day, with the examining light on us, we're something different. But once the lights are switched off, we revert to ourselves to breathlessly share the secrets of the day.

I do it a lot with Clarisse. She's my new doll, and a friend. She's just like the old one, who never got a name because I didn't have her long enough. Even the red hair is the same. Saša got her for me when I told him about the other one that Mother said was lost.

I named her Clarisse because I saw it in a magazine once and liked the sound of it. I thought if a Raggedy Ann had a name like that she'd be suddenly transformed into a radiant princess with golden hair, and I could spend all day combing it and talking to her about what it was like to be a princess.

The change never happened, though we were able to

SARAJEVO

talk about anything. I knew how she would feel if I held her up to the mirror, with her stringy red hair and her blank face, so I refrained from doing so. Why punish her? Most often I held her in my lap and thought of her as a sister: we're so alike.

I left her propped against a pillow on the bed so she could look out a window and entertain herself while I was gone. Now I want to run to her, across the courtyard and into the silent emptiness of the ruined building. I desperately need to know she's safe amid the crumbling bricks that are an embarrassment to what was once our home.

I want Luka to be here, to offer me his hand. But he'd only scoff at me for my fears and my trembling, saying, "She's only a doll." The thought of his rejection makes me wish instead for the quiet of Omar and his acceptance in the dark.

I don't remember crossing the courtyard or entering the building. All at once I'm inside. The cat followed me in, thinking, I guess, that I would protect and feed it. But that's not the way I feel at all. The sight of the confused rubble makes me fiercely angry. I have no one else to take it out on, so I hiss at the cat, stomping my feet and chasing it away. I'm not satisfied until it goes into hiding among the mess and clutter. Then I still wish I could find it and chase it outside.

I'm afraid to go to our flat. We're on the second floor, in the back. Mother said it was handy because there was a fire escape and she could hang the wash there easily.

HOTEL

Once I found her there singing, which was not like her, as she straightened the clothes over the railing. It was when Saša first came.

There's only the one bedroom. That night Mother led me by the hand to the couch in the living room. I held my blanket and Clarisse in my other hand. Mother sat with me for a moment, smiling and saying, "You're a big girl now." But I didn't feel like a big girl when she got up to leave, tousling my hair, and when the bedroom door closed behind her I only felt alone.

In a minute I could hear Saša's laughter and hers in reply, and then I was even more alone and humiliated. I turned on my side and held Clarisse tighter. I wanted to run to the room and yell at them to look at me, to really look at me to see that I was worth noises too, not just silence. But wanting to cry, I only sank deeper into my covers. I told myself I must be brave for Clarisse, so I kissed her and covered her face till we both slept. It was only much later I knew that they hadn't been laughing at me.

In front of our flat, I'm surprised the door's still standing intact. I start to knock, not wanting to interrupt anything.

I don't know what I expect to find. I'm afraid Mother will come running out with fire in her hair. My hand hesitates on the door before I push it slowly open.

I'm relieved to find the flat empty. When I let out a deep breath, I know what I'd been worried about. I'd been

58

afraid I'd find their bodies there, that I'd be alone with their staring eyes.

I've seen dead bodies before, but that was in the street and they were strangers who stared back at me without seeing. It would be different and horrifying to find in your own flat someone you knew staring at you like that.

Dead eyes are begging eyes. That's the quality I'll always associate with them. They beg us, the living, to give them back their lives. I always feel useless looking at them and quickly turn away.

I don't want my eyes to be that way. I prefer to think they'll be smiling, or anyway just flat and blank like Clarisse's.

I'm calm to find myself alone. The living room and kitchen look practically the same; there's only the bedroom to be concerned about.

I'm hungry. I'd forgotten about eating till now.

In the kitchen everything is in place, except for some scattered debris from the ceiling. There's one chair turned over on its side like someone quickly got up and let it fall, but the other is just standing there waiting.

Now the rocket shows we watched from the courtyard of the Sarajevo aren't so pretty to think of anymore. One of them visited here and perhaps took Mother and Saša away. Now I miss them, even their silences and disinterest. If that's all you have, it's better than nothing at all.

I'm worried about Clarisse. She should be there in the bedroom, but I'm not ready to go there yet. Instead I concentrate on being hungry and nose around to see what I can find. The tiny refrigerator is dead, with its door ajar. The smell of rancid cheese makes me turn away, and I kick the door as I would have liked to kick the cat. Mother was never one for cooking, making an effort only because I was there, then later because Saša was always hungry when he came.

The breadbox is still covered on the counter. Brushing some pieces of plaster off it hopefully, I pause before opening it. I like bread when it's fresh and warm, but Mother always scolded me for going to the box and pinching some off before a meal. But there's no one here to scold me now, just the quiet, so I free the top of the box and stick my eager hand in, as though I expect to find bread just out of the oven waiting for me.

The bread is hard and crusty, but still good. It takes both hands to break off a piece with a *snap!* that sounds loud and out of place. It makes me look quickly around to see who made it.

I dust off the chair that's standing, then sit. I hear myself say out loud, "Please, is anyone here?" I'm embarrassed at that, and quickly, to get rid of it, I set the other chair upright next to me to have some company.

What a comfort it would be to hold Clarisse and talk to her! I look longingly at the bedroom door, then away. What if the rocket flashes left Mother and Saša there waiting like the chairs? That's how they'd be, I'm sure: apart from one another and at different angles, like they'd pushed away at the last moment, fleeing. They'd not be locked arm in arm like the dead lovers. Mother never had the quality of closeness, and I don't think Saša did either, for all his noise. I've only had it with Clarisse, but I'd like to with Luka.

With a jump, the cat appears in the window. Then I remember I left the door to the flat open and I go to close it, followed by the silence. I pass the closed door of the bedroom again, that I've been avoiding, and wonder why it's closed. Was someone going in, for safety, or coming out, in escape? Either way it seems a useless gesture.

I know I can't leave without opening the door, and I'm beginning to think myself a coward for not going to it and pushing it open resolutely. I'm glad Luka's not here to see me.

Facing the bedroom door, my heart is beating so hard that I'd like to scream to make it stop, but dare not. Not because someone might hear, but because it would be an admission of my helplessness. And then how could I go on?

I'm going to open the door now, in a minute.

When I'm ready.

There's a bookcase still standing against the wall, though the few books and the knickknacks that Mother liked to collect have been mostly knocked to the floor. There's the ceramic lion, painted and once so proudly roaring. Now it's lying on its side with the head staring at a silly, useless angle, the snarl still on its lips. It used to scare me. I asked Mother about lions and she said there were none in Sarajevo, only in zoos. That reassured me

and I was able to approach the lion and grin back at it, trying to roar myself. The lion prepared me for Saša and his
noise. Often I thought of him as a lion, only friendly.
That way we got along.

Our photo album is on the floor too. It's fallen open to
the only picture I really like of myself. It was taken just
before the start of the war. It makes me look older and
more confident, and there's something of a smile, too,
that I like. Above my picture is what Mother liked to call
a "family photo." Saša is in the middle with Mother at his
side. I'm second from right next to Saša. That's Jasmina
beside me. The others Mother rounded up from the
neighborhood to make a group. She was afraid there
wouldn't be enough of us for a proper photo.

Also on the floor is a framed photo. It's turned away
from me, but I know what it is. It's of Mother and Saša. I
took it. Smiling, Saša said, "One, two . . ." then just as I
snapped it he pinched Mother from behind, making her
jump, and that's the picture I got.

I pick up the picture to see if they're still smiling, and
they are, although the glass has been shattered. I put it
back on the shelf and then everything is almost as before.
I leave the album where it is because I like the fact that
chance opened it to my picture.

Opening the door wasn't so hard. After I put the picture
back I went to the door and opened it without thinking,
though at the last I thought of Luka.

Mother and Saša are not here. Somehow they've escaped. Clarisse, however, wasn't so lucky. I found her on the floor under the broken window.

She's lost an arm that I can't find, but otherwise she's okay. She's glad to see me, I can tell. After all our time together she can talk to me without speaking.

She's happy now to be cradled in my arms. There's glass covering the bed, so I sit on the floor near the window where I found her. For me the bed still contains Mother's and Saša's noises, so Clarisse and I wouldn't feel right there. Anyway, I'm more comfortable in the light from the window.

I want her to tell me everything that's happened, but she's reluctant to do so. She's not afraid; I know she'll come around to it in her own time, when she's ready.

I'm not worried about Mother and Saša, only wondering where they've got to. There are shelters scattered around the city, but I don't think they've gone to one of those. Saša would be too proud. Somehow they've made out and when things settle down and there's no more shelling, they'll come for me. But maybe with the building in its ruined state they'd not think to look for me here, and they know nothing of my life at the Sarajevo.

It's just myself and Clarisse. She's beginning to be a little frightened: her eyes are getting larger. I reach under the bed and find her brush where I left it and comb out her tangled hair.

She's still embarrassed, I see, about the arm. It must be awkward to have just the one arm. People probably would laugh, like the boys laughed in the street at Mira. Why

HOTEL

is it always men who laugh at such things, and never women? Maybe they know something we don't. I've seen Luka laugh like that; and in the hospital he and Ilija and Adnan all laughed.

Clarisse and I are shaking because of a draft coming in through the window. Then I hum to both of us, some nonsense tune I make up as I go along.

We're getting cold, so I take Clarisse with me back to the other room to my little sofa bed and my blanket, where we can be comfortable. I don't want to spend the night in the flat, but there's no choice. It's too dark to make my way back to the Sarajevo. Clarisse doesn't notice as I brush the dust and plaster off the sofa. In the morning we'll finish the stick of bread together.

I'll make her another arm one day. Then she'll be good as new.

As I drift away to sleep, I try to think of Luka, but can't. Instead I'm in the sanctuary with the candles and the dead lovers. Then I see the dark of Omar's eyes inviting me, and my lips form themselves into a quiet smile.

IN THE MORNING CLARISSE IS AWAKE BEFORE ME. I want to take her with me back to the Sarajevo, but know I can't. I'd only be laughed at, and she would be too, for her missing arm. I couldn't stand for her to be made fun of, so I brush her hair again, that she likes, and find her an out-of-the-way place in the bedroom. I leave her sitting in a corner on the floor next to the dresser. She stares at me, making me feel guilty for not taking her along. So I tell her joyfully that I'll come back for her one day.

Outside, the fresh air hurries me along. My hair blowing back seems to carry the past with it, and I feel lighter, as though I'm floating toward the future.

I'm almost to the Sarajevo when I'm drawn to the Turkish quarter on the hill. Omar will be there. When he left me outside the sanctuary of the dead lovers with, "Well, good-bye then," suddenly good-bye wasn't enough. I couldn't stand the sound of it, wanted no more of it. I secretly followed him down the Vojvode Stepe, through the Boščaršija, then up the narrow streets climbing the hill to the old district, where I watched him disappear into a house.

HOTEL

So now my feet already know the way. Going to him, I have the same quiet feeling of acceptance I felt in the sanctuary, where he'd seemed to drift into the candle-light, then away, so that the only real sense I had of his presence was that of light and dark.

As I round the corner of the old stone warehouse across from his building, he's there in the doorway, smiling. He looks just as I left him, and I have to rub my eyes to make sure I haven't been here all night. By that time he's crossed the street to me.

I'm afraid he'll actually think I've waited through the night for him, but he only says, "Are you hungry?" as though we'd made a date for breakfast. The fluttering of my stomach admits that I am, and he takes my hand without asking and leads me off down the hill.

I'm intensely conscious of his hand, its enveloping softness, even though I don't look at him. Instead, my eyes are fixed to the point, far off, where the sky and the rising mists off the Miljacka meet one another, mixing together like our hands, which seems just that natural.

After a minute I completely forget our hands are together, and, if he had dropped mine, it would have felt strange to have it hanging alone, useless.

I like the lines of his face. They're strong without being sharp, and his eyes, though still deep, are not serious as in the dark of the sanctuary, but laughing with the day.

"I knew you'd come," he says, and that makes me lower my eyes. I don't think he notices, because he puts his arm around my shoulder like we're old friends. It's not heavy at all, just resting. I'm thinking of Clarisse in the corner of the flat, afraid she's lonely, but when his arm befriends me I forget all about her and let myself go with him.

A tight little shell breaks from around me where I was holding myself in, but instead of being afraid I rush happily to meet the sun with a smile, thrilling at my freedom.

I'm glad I've come today to exchange smiles with Omar. I wish I could find a friend for Clarisse so she could do the same.

We're under the canvas awning of a kiosk and, though others are crowded around us, pushing and shoving, I feel us alone. Then Omar kisses me, so quick I don't know it's coming.

It's nothing like I'd expected. He doesn't put his tongue in my mouth like I'd seen Radman do with Jan. He simply touches his lips softly against mine and rests them there for a moment. Except for his warmth, I could have been kissed by a flower or the morning breeze. Not being prepared to be kissed, I forget to close my eyes, and my big eyes must look strange staring directly into his when he opens them. But Omar doesn't seem to notice; he's off again, whistling.

"Where are we going?" I ask. It sounds strange after I've said it, because I don't care as long as I have his company.

"Breakfast."

"Have you any money?"

He turns out his empty pockets for me to see.

"How'll we manage?" I'm becoming very conscious of

the noises from my stomach. Instead of answering, Omar
rubs my hair and pulls me after him down street after narrow street, further into the Turkish quarter than I've
ever been.

We come to a fountain in a square at the end of a
twisted street that has no outlet. On the other side of the
stone square is a large pink house with Moorish columns
and a tiled roof. It's been spared the shelling. There's a
wrought iron fence around the front, guarding it.

"Who belongs here?" I ask Omar. I can see gardens inside the fence. I'm amazed that such a beautiful, fantas-
tic place can exist, untouched by the war.

"My friend Kemal lives here. You'll see."

I squeeze through the fence after Omar, who moves
aside a broken iron spear like he knows it's there.

We go through the garden by a narrow path, around to
the back of the house. We're like explorers among the
thickness of the plants, which reach out their friendly
hands to touch our faces. Their waving fingers are cool,
moist, and inviting. I like to let myself be led by Omar,
without a thought as to where we're going.

When we come out of the garden there's a covered terrace before us. It's open, with arches. The floor is made
up of brilliant blue tiles with mosaics worked into it to
form patterns. I'm so intent on trying to discover the nature of the designs that I don't see the young boy seated
straight and quiet behind the carved wooden table. Then
I hear Omar say, "Here's Kemal."

He's in the shadows and it takes a moment for me to

SARAJEVO

know that his eyes cannot see mine. I squeeze Omar's hand tightly, and he squeezes back. But as soon as I hear Kemal's voice I'm okay.

"So, you've come after all."

"I've brought a friend." Omar pushes me forward for Kemal's inspection. That doesn't seem odd in the least, so I stand relaxed before him.

"My name is Alma." He didn't ask me, but his expression seemed to want to know.

"You have a beautiful voice," Kemal says. "I imagine you beautiful." Kemal's words are like a smile surrounding me.

Omar is pleased at my acceptance, and for my part I want to rush forward and thank Kemal with both arms around him in a hug, but hold myself back.

"We're hungry."

Kemal smiles at my boldness.

"Come, join me." He pulls back the chair next to him and I'm quick to sit down.

Kemal leans over to me as if he's trying to smell me, and says, "Give me your hand," which I do as soon as he asks for it. He puts his other hand on top of mine, and now both his hands are looking at me, discovering me. I'm not afraid to look at his eyes. They aren't vacant or staring, only contemplative.

He's lucky to have such calm eyes. Mine aren't calm, just detached. There are times when I like them that way and others when I don't. It was okay when I walked in on Mother and Saša, or when I looked at the dead lovers, but not when I saw Luka with his arm around Sandra. Then the emotion quickly rose up inside me to my eyes, and they weren't detached at all, but wide and burning.

I envy Kemal his eyes and am curious about them. I want to ask if it's because of an accident or was he born with them. I don't think he would have minded my asking, but instead, because of his smallness behind the table against the vastness of the house, I ask, "Are you all alone here?"

In answer he smiles again, then calls out loudly, "Medina!" In a moment a plump little old woman with a colored scarf around her head enters from a door that by the smell it lets out must give onto the kitchen. My hunger deepens as the door opens, then closes.

Waiting silently with a dishrag in her hands, Medina stands behind Kemal.

Kemal says, "Some breakfast for my friends. Turska kava, and some ćevapčići."

My stomach growls at the thought of the coffee that I know will be steaming, and the tiny grilled sausages filled with onions and peppers. I know they'll be today's, not warmed over from the day before, and I'm jealous at that. Mother always saved scraps of everything and gave it back to us the next morning, cold. If the day before had been unpleasant or lonely, that quality carried over in the food, and it seemed sad to be eaten again.

There's nothing sad about Kemal. Even when he's not smiling, his face looks like it's getting ready to smile. Perhaps he's never had warmed-over food. I look intently at the corners of his mouth, at the smile lines there; then Medina returns and places a steaming plate before me. My stomach growls again and I start to dive in but stop and glance at Omar. His eyes say wait. Then he says respectfully, "We appreciate your generosity," which Kemal's laugh accepts. My mouth is already full—how good the hot taste of the food!—when I hear Kemal say, "I am pleased to have you with me."

We eat in silence. My plate is cleaned first, and Kemal says, "There are figs in the garden if you like." By the tone of his voice I know it's a dismissal. He and Omar have male secrets to share alone, like Luka and Dejan. But I don't mind; I want to explore.

I jump off the terrace and head down the stone-flagged path through the garden. After I go a little distance, something makes me turn around to look, but the path has taken a turn and all I can see is the red-tiled roof of the house over the trees—nothing of the terrace. For a second I'm afraid I've imagined the whole thing, afraid even that there is no Omar or Kemal, that I'm back in the flat or the Sarajevo. Then I feel the fronds of the plants caressing my face and the happy fullness of my stomach, and I know it's real.

In the trees ahead of me there's a yellow, singing bird. I run after it. It hears me coming and flies, settling on another branch where I disturb it again. I give myself up to this little game. There's only the garden and the bird and, miraculously, the sound of my own laughter, that I'm not guilty for.

HOTEL

After a while the bird and I both tire. It sits watching me while turning its head from side to side, trying to decide what sort of creature I am.

I plop down on the ground under a fig tree, and the heavy ripeness of the fruit invites me to pick it. I've never before known anyone who owned fig trees. With Mother, I was content with a few sticks of furniture and a change of clothes. How different to have a whole garden with fig trees!

The fruit is plump, juicy, and sweet. One could remain here forever in the garden, living only on figs, and never have to leave. That thought fills me, and I eat and eat until I want no more. Then I fall back upon the soft fragrance of the grass, my face warmed by the sun, catching glimpses of clouds moving through holes in the branches. I want to sleep.

I don't know how long I've been lying here.

There's a dull sound, far off. It sounds like thunder but I don't want to open my eyes.

Then quickly I'm afraid. I run through the trees toward the house, my face stinging from the vines hitting at me, trying to hold me back. I'm afraid that Omar and Kemal will be taken by the sounds, as Mother and Saša were.

For a moment I'm lost in the garden; then I'm on the path leading to the house and I'm out of breath. As soon as I turn the corner there's Omar waving to Kemal, thanking him. I run to Omar and grab for his hand, and when I do the rumblings stop.

As Omar leads me away, I want another look at Kemal, so just as we reach the fence I turn back and wave. Even though I haven't spoken, Kemal calls out, "Come back when you can."

I duck my head to go through the fence and we're gone, but long after that I can still see the calmness of his eyes.

PART
TWO

I T'S ALMOST DAWN. It's a time I've always associated with myself. You can feel the sun coming before it's there. Then suddenly it is there and you're warm all over. I've always thought of the dawn as a kiss, or a promise.

We left the Sarajevo while it was still dark. Luka decided it was the best time to attack the Centrals in their own place and put a real scare into them. That would establish our superiority over them, he said.

Shapes move about me in the half-light. One shape is Ilija, another is Dejan. I don't see Luka's shape, but I know he's there, somewhere beyond the line of light and dark. The thought of his presence, even unseen, comforts me.

One shape, small and timid, comes closer and I can smell the sweat and the fear of Milorad in the hot stickiness of the dying summer night. I know he'd rather be safe and quiet back in his corner of the courtyard at the Sarajevo. They've brought him along, Luka says, to make a man of him, but I know that he'll always remain a child. I'd like to hold him and brush back his hair, and with it his fear, but that would only make the others laugh if they saw, so I leave him to suffer in his own perplexity.

HOTEL

I know he doesn't really understand. He doesn't understand the need for this raid on the Centrals, just as he doesn't understand the rocks in his hands that he must fling at them to assure his place with Ilija and the rest. It's expected of him, that's all he knows. If I could see his eyes now, I bet they'd be large and quizzical, just as they were when they looked at me in the shower, or when I kissed his cheek on the stairs, knowing it would make him run away.

Only he can't run away now. He has to go through with it and at least appear to be brave, or be branded a coward by the others and suffer their endless taunts.

I'm sorry now I called out to him, "Milorad is a 'fraidy cat!" Perhaps he's thinking of it now and that's what is causing him to sweat, more than any apprehension he has about the raid.

I'm glad he saw me in the shower, glad also that I didn't turn my body away from his gaze, but allowed him his pleasure in looking. I wish I could do it for him again, right now, if that would take his fear away.

I should be honored, I guess, to be here with them, my shape mixed with theirs in the dark. I'm the only girl who's ever been allowed on a raid. There's perhaps twenty of us here now. A few of the boys were left with the other girls in the Sarajevo.

It's only because of a lark, one of Luka's moods. When I spoke up, telling him I would take Milorad's place, the others only laughed. But Luka looked at me for a long time and then said, "Both of you will come," putting an end to it. And immediately afterward, when it sank in, I felt a sudden, thrilling rush to be included, perhaps because his words stopped the others' laughter. I was surprised at first at my courage at speaking to Luka in such a way, but then I looked at Milorad's face and saw the relief spreading over it and I was glad.

I don't know what Luka was thinking when he decided I should come with them. Perhaps he saw a challenge to his authority and felt the easiest way to put it down was to make it his own idea. All that day and into the night the thought kept creeping silently up into me that maybe he actually wanted me to be there with him, for some reason known only to himself. That thought both excited and scared me.

Now I feel Luka's eyes in the semi-darkness, even though I can't see them. But his shape is there, having moved in front of me, and in the moment he stands there motionless, the light comes and then I can see his eyes. They're watching mine to see if they're afraid, and I'm glad that they're not. He turns and is gone, shouting to Dejan and Ilija.

The purpose of this raid, Luka says, is to gain supplies—and drugs if they have any—but I don't think that's the real reason. They just have the need to show off, like Saša with Mother.

Only Milorad is not that way at all. He's there behind the others, hesitant as usual, like their shadow. Maybe that's what it is to be a poet. Maybe that does not require words.

When Milorad used to tell me he'd be a poet when he was grown I'd laughed inwardly so he couldn't see. I'd thought of a poet as a leader, powerful, like Luka, like the sun, whose words would be rays to warm you and make you want to follow. But now, watching him inching along against the side of the building as though seeking to vanish into the cracks of the stone, I know how wrong I was. I'd not seen what he meant at all. He was very like a shadow in his confusion and his pain. His purpose was to exist behind—a dark, elongated whisper that followed after, pulling at you gently. The sun is only a happy feel; you can see nothing looking directly into it. Whereas if you happened to cast a glance behind you or alongside, depending on the angle, and studied your shadow, so like yourself but different too, then you could learn something. That's what poetry is, I decide, and I begin to see Milorad in a new light.

I was sorry for him before. I was sorry for his smallness and his fear. I was sorry that he'd been ordered to take part in the raid, a witness to their senseless antics. But now I see his presence as a necessary reminder, like Clarisse's missing arm or Kemal's sightless eyes. They're all reminders. I'm no longer worried over Clarisse. She's powerful in her poetry just as Milorad is in his. I get closer to him in the rising light, hoping our shadows will flow together and be one.

SARAJEVO

Luka shouts again, then Ilija and the rest. They've broken through the door and driven back the single guard, useless to stop them in their frenzy. They burst through the lobby shouting, "Death to the Centrals!" flinging their rocks at anything and everything, but making more noise than anything else. The sounds of the rocks mixed with their screams are like the shells bursting from the hills—they too scream before they hit—and I'm a little dizzy and sick at my stomach.

Milorad grips his rocks tightly in his hands. I want to shout out to him. His eyes find mine and are full of a pain that wants to run away, but can't.

In his desperation he flings his handful of rocks against a gigantic wall mirror that shatters with a resounding *crack!*, causing a cheer to go up among the Jevos. Dejan, all smiles, pats him on the back, making him one of them. Milorad won't even look at me, but runs down the hall after the others. He's silent, not screaming, but contained in their screams nonetheless.

I'm glad I don't feel the need to scream as they do. It must be a tremendous release, however. That must be the real reason for the raid—to let out their pent-up screams.

Once, in the winter, I heard a story about an old woman from Jablanica who'd been horribly raped before she was killed. I shivered when I heard it told, and now I do again, knowing she must have closed her ears to their screams as she held in her own, like Milorad. I'd like to stuff my fingers in my ears to drown out their lusty screams with my crying ones, but don't because of what Luka and the others would think if they saw me.

I'm worried about Milorad and start down a corridor to look for him. They've caught the Centrals off guard, and Luka won't be satisfied with simply snatching some food and blankets, then bolting. He'll want to shake them up a bit. I can hear them from the direction of the kitchen at the end of the dining hall, and more shouts from the floors above. There's total confusion in the dark; like us, the Centrals are without electricity now too.

At the end of the hall Dejan pops through the swinging double doors to the kitchen with a small sack of rice in his hands and a piece of bread sticking from his mouth, making him look bizarre, but funny at the same time. But he doesn't concern me now. I only ask flatly, "Where's Milorad?" Dejan's eyes only smile and laugh in answer, then he darts past me down a long corridor with his laughter trailing behind him.

His look has scared me. I've seen it before in the eyes of fresh troops on their way to the front lines. I follow him, uneasy, but compelled for Milorad's sake.

I hear shouts from one of the rooms. What game are they playing at now? Their laughter is raucous and has a mean sound to it.

That recalls a trip I made once with Mother, before Saša and the war. It was to Rodoc, a modest little town to the north. We went to see an aunt who was dying. We took the train. At the station there was a wagon of gypsies. The wagon was bright red, and one man had a bear on a leash. The bear had a muzzle that allowed him to drink, and was downing glass after glass of ker to the great amusement of the spectators. They really got going when the bear stopped and belched. His helplessness was funny to them. To me, however, they were the ones who should be pitied and laughed at. I can still see their flat, stupid, unfeeling faces. I wanted to run at them, kicking them and screaming at them to stop. There was a gypsy woman crouching over a fire near the wagon, cooking. She raised her head and looked at me sadly, continuing to stir at the pot. I felt in her gaze not her sympathy but her sameness. She too was forced to turn away, helpless, at the swift and violent sight of their arrogance and pride. At that moment, when our eyes met, I felt myself becoming a woman.

At the door of the room there's the same unchanging sound of their shouts and laughter from within, as with the bear-baiters. But I have to go in because of Milorad. I'm afraid the others will push him without remorse into the cold hard light and remove his shadow from him forever. Then he'll never be a poet. He'll be forced into a world where the baiting of bears is not only allowed, but thought funny. The laughers don't know what it's like. The humiliating sound of it enters every pore of your body, causing you to see yourself as they see you, and that's worst of all.

Opening the door, I find Milorad exposed by the light from the double French windows, whose curtains have

HOTEL

been ripped down. The others are at their fun. Most I never allow names because I can't stand their boorishness. They've formed a circle around Milorad. I'd like to break through them and rescue him, but Luka is there, slightly apart from the rest, staring at me coldly.

A big laugh goes up; then someone shouts, "Out with it now! Don't be shy!"

Milorad, in the middle of the laughing circle, is the victim of their prank. His pants are around his ankles and he's standing in his shorts, shivering. His hands are open and useless at his sides. I make myself look at his face. His lips are pressed together tightly, and his timid and pained eyes are drawn reluctantly by the force of Luka's presence to the frightened young girl Ilija and Dejan are holding against the bed. Nenad is there also, but his hands aren't holding her, only his eternal mask of silence, that's perhaps even more scary.

I wish I had eyes like Kemal's. Or I wish I could clap my hands for silence, and in the quiet there would be nothing of fear or want or pain or desire. Then I could spirit Milorad away before the others noticed, back to the safety of his corner in the courtyard with only his shadow against the wall. Only then would I clap my hands again, releasing them to go about their business without requiring his presence.

The girl is fully clothed, so I don't know if they're just playing or not. Her face is like mine was on Zuc. Through their laughter, I can hear her muffled sobs. The unprotected sounds only set them off more. They push Milorad forward, duck-walking with his pants down. One of them shouts, "She's waiting for you!"

I pray for Milorad swiftly, but, against my prayers, he takes a step forward. And just that one hesitant step is enough to mark his shame.

I hear her sobbing again, that's broken by a laugh, anonymous and cutting. Then I don't care about Luka's eyes or anything else, but rush to help Milorad, with my hands and feet hitting against the wall of their laughter. I hit one of them on the shoulder and feel a rush of pride at his yelp of pain. I'm pushed back and down, but I don't register the hurt as I hit the floor.

I start to get up to fight them again, but's there's a shrill whistle down the hall, then the mad rushing of feet and the shout again, "Death to the Centrals!" Then everything goes crazy. There're blows, one on my shoulder that smarts, but I can think only of Milorad. Reaching out my hands stupidly, expecting to find him, I call his name. And that's like magic, because his shaking hands are suddenly in mine. We're so close I can see his sick eyes. With more strength than I thought myself capable of, I pull him away and drag him through the crowd and shouts and blows.

Outside the room we're free and running down the corridor. There are more shouts, following us, and I run harder with him up the stairs where there's quiet for a moment before the shouts break on us again. We're at the end of a corridor with only a window in front of us and the shouts pursuing. I shove him out the window and onto the fire escape, the hard, cold steel greeting us ominously.

Milorad's eyes ask me if I've seen his shame, and mine can't lie. The shouts are at the window behind us, and hands too, grabbing for us. Vladan's angry, contorted face pops up in the window, like a figure from a shooting gallery at a fair. I can't hear the obscenities I know his moving mouth makes in the shape of hate itself—because I can't blame him for them.

I push Milorad down the ladder and he hangs there pathetically, not knowing what to do when he's removed from his shadow.

I shout to him, "Jump!" He looks down and then lets go, disappearing as though falling through a mirror that doesn't shatter. I can't see him below, but I hear a soft cry, then nothing.

Then I'm retreating, falling down the ladder too, away from their grasping hands. I don't look up at them again. I don't want to see their faces. When I reach the end of the ladder, I let go and fall freely to the ground.

Frightened, Milorad is struggling to rise. We're being pelted by rocks as I jerk him up. They keep buckets of them handy at the windows.

I start to run but he falls again, crying out, "My leg!" Amid the rocks and the insults flung our way, my hand touches his leg and comes away wet. I taste it and it's blood.

With my arm around him, we hobble down the alley as

SARAJEVO

best we can. The Centrals won't follow because of a possible ambush.

I don't remember much after that, except that the sound of their laughter ringing in my ears hurt more, much more, than any of the rocks striking me.

Later, back in Milorad's sheltered corner of the courtyard, where even the daylight is not sharp because of the height of the walls and the sycamore, he sobs only a little bit, then goes to sleep against me.

I lay his head gently aside on a patch of grass and, taking up a broken spoon lying in the dirt near the tree, I begin methodically and without feeling to erase the marks of my name on the tree, until you can no longer tell whose it had once been.

M ILORAD IS SICK. I don't think it's bad. After the
raid, when I had a chance to examine his leg,
it was covered with blood. I got a little water in a bucket
and washed it carefully. He whimpered the whole time,
even though I tried my best not to hurt him. There was a
brownish streak over the cut, like rust. He must have
scraped his leg on a piece of pipe as he fell.

We have no bandages, so when I finished I spit in my
hand, then rubbed it over the cut, saying brightly, "All
better now!" I'd heard somewhere that it was good for
healing and would protect you.

I was afraid they would taunt him about the girl. Actually, it's just the reverse. He's a hero of sorts because of his
wound. The attack of the Centrals came so soon after he
took a step toward the girl that they think he heard the
whistle and was rushing to the attack as he broke out of
the circle. Only he and I know the truth.

It bothers me to see Milorad basking in their praise.
Ilija slapped him on the back with "Well done!" Even Dejan, who's usually reserved, asked to see his wound and
complimented him on it. I wanted him to stay in bed and
rest, but after the Princess Sandra came to congratulate

him, he would have none of it, limping about all over the place to receive their smiles and acceptance. I told him he was showing off and he frowned and flung back at me, "What do you know anyway; you're only a girl," so I left him alone.

One day he insisted on carrying water up to all the rooms himself. I could see the pain on his face even though he tried to hide it.

Luka's changed. There's not the same laughter. Everything, even the war, used to be a joke to him. When they used to return to the Sarajevo after a raid, he would take up the lid of the trash can that was his throne and beat it loudly, proclaiming, "I am the chief because I am the strongest!" and no one dared dispute him. A few weeks after the raid where Milorad hurt his leg, however, Luka was seen talking to a man in the street. After that he wandered off and didn't return until the next day. Then, as though exhausted, he went silently to his room and stayed there for a long time.

When finally he came out, he was his old self again, smiling broadly and calling to Ilija, "Some dinner for your chief!" That made Ilija happy, and he rushed about to bring him some bread and cold rice, which Luka lordly accepted. But there was something different in his eyes and around the corners of his mouth, something hard that I didn't understand.

It was only later that the rest of us learned that Vladan had been killed by a sniper. It was a stupid end to him:

he'd failed to run across Sniper's Alley! When I heard it, I worried about who would protect Maud. Our war with the Centrals was over because there was no one strong enough to take Vladan's place.

Then I realized that what I'd seen in Luka's eyes was fear, that was never there before.

I love him, though. I know I still love him. I must.

Now I meet Omar regularly, though it was never talked over or planned out.

We've been meeting in an abandoned store halfway between his place and the Sarajevo. We found it by accident, ducking in there one day when it started to rain, a real downpour. We discovered it had a back room that was quite dry and cozy. Omar dragged a mattress in from the alley and we proudly called the room "our home."

We lay together on the mattress, I somewhat stiffly and he with his arm across my breasts. I liked the heavy comfort of it, and I amused myself staring at patterns in the broken ceiling.

Omar never talks about himself, and that leaves him a mystery, which both attracts me and makes me afraid. I started to question him the first day we lay on the mattress, but he only said, "Do you want me to go?" So I kept quiet and allowed him to unbutton my dress to put his hands in, but that's as far as we went.

When he touched me there I felt guilty because of Luka, though I had the presence of mind not to pull back. Instead I closed my eyes and didn't let myself think at all.

SARAJEVO

Then his hands became hands not attached to a person. They were just there for me as I was there for them, and it was alright.

Later, when Omar rose to go, my breasts were suddenly frightened and insecure without the protection of his arm.

That night, back in the Sarajevo, alone in the dark I removed my clothes and, lying on the mattress without any cover, crossed my arms over my breasts to try to get the same feel, but it was no good. Maybe it's because his arm is heavier and his hands have a heavy, male smell about them.

All at once I was completely isolated and unprotected. I was afraid there was nothing beyond the dark—no hotel, no Luka, no Mother and Saša—and I even didn't exist. I wanted to cry, but instead buried my head against the mattress and stuffed the cover into my mouth until the fear went away to sleep.

In the morning when I woke, it was already light. There was a spot of blood on the mattress. Then I found it on my clothes too, between my legs. For a second I was scared I'd been wounded somehow, like Milorad. Then a real smile spread across my face. I kicked back the cover, wishing Mother were here so I could tell her and show her I'd finally got my period.

That had always worried her. From when I was eleven or twelve she'd expected it all the time, so that the importance she attached to it worried me also. She'd mull over it for a while, then say, "It's the stress of things," or, "You can blame it on the war," or finally, "You're just late, that's all," so that I didn't know what to think, only that I was lacking in some way that upset her.

If she'd been here I could have shown her the spot with pride, and she'd have wanted to hug me and make a fuss over me, that she never did before. But there was no one to tell.

All that day, however, everyone seemed to notice a difference in me as I hummed softly to myself while going about my chores in the Sarajevo. Even Milorad, though he had a fever and his leg hurt, smiled at me and said, "What's gotten into you today?"

I could hardly wait to meet Omar and give him the happy news. It couldn't have come at a better time. Now I'd be a real woman for him.

When I finished up and went outside, there was Milorad coming up the steps again to annoy me. He was limping in a pair of shoes much too big for him. God knows where he got them. I laughed at him because of the shoes, a pair of ugly, floppy blue sneakers.

I called to him, "Let me borrow your shoes."

"Why?" He bravely tried to hide the pain from his leg.

"I want to make soup!"

With that he rushed at me in mock anger that didn't fool me. Then he stumbled, catching himself with his hands on the railing, and I didn't laugh at him again.

I left him on the steps looking after me. He looked so forlorn that, if it hadn't been for Omar waiting, I'd have rushed back to him and tickled him all the way to the courtyard. We would sit in the corner and make up stories to tell each other, like we once did. Mostly they were harmless, things we'd invented, giving ourselves grand parts to downplay the fact that without the Sarajevo, we'd be nothing. Once, however, we came to the courtyard at the same time, drawn together. We were both shaking a little, though each tried to hide it. It was about a story we'd heard in the street. It was true, they said.

The town of Srebrenica had been split down the middle by the war into Serb and Muslim. I can't tell about the things they did to one another. A boy, a soldier but very young, was caught by the other side. They taunted him; then, laughing, they beat him savagely in the middle of the square. They set him on fire and watched him burn, like we sit in the courtyard at night and watch the flashes from the rockets. I wondered if his screams were like those of the rockets—high, shrill, and hopeless.

They said when his mother heard of it she came to the door of her stone hut, whose roof had been badly damaged by shelling, and stared blankly at a group of happy soldiers on their way to the front line. When one raised his cap to her, she screamed out, "Damn this country! Damn this war!" and spit on the ground, a silent curse to them all.

It was the thought of the flames that scared me the most. Once, during a time of heavy shelling when all you could hear were the angry noises, Mother put her arms around me and held me close, not for me, but for herself. She shook and mumbled that Sarajevo was like Sodom and Gomorrah and would surely be destroyed by fire.

HOTEL

Later I asked Radman what she'd meant, and he only laughed and said we'd done nothing wrong and it was more likely to be our Golgotha, so I was still confused.

Now I lie on the mattress waiting for Omar. There's a fly buzzing against the window, trying to get out. The window isn't broken because the front of the store is intact. The backside is rubble, and the fly has only to flee in that direction and it's free. But he continues to beat himself against the imprisoning glass, making that horrible, frantic, buzz-buzzing sound. If you amplified it thousands of times that would be the sound of Sarajevo, of its people running in the streets to avoid the sniper fire. I imagine myself throwing my body recklessly, with abandon, against an unbreakable window of despair, and my screams are not words but only long-drawn-out, wailing bbbzzzes.

The fly stops for a second and looks at me. He's a friend, and I softly enclose him in my hand, then carry him to the open rear of the store and set him free. He doesn't accept it immediately; then he flies away.

It's uncomfortable in the open, so I go back inside. There's something quiet and cool about the dark that I like. Dark makes alone alright and easier to bear.

My heart is pounding but the rest of me is calm as I wait for Omar. Having become used to his hands, I'm not afraid anymore. I haven't let him go any further than touching, but now I trust him to stay, and I want us to be intimate. We're young, but the war speeds things up.

SARAJEVO

Sometimes he brings me little things, whatever he can manage. It might be a tomato or a handful of figs. Only I don't like for him to bring figs anymore. The last time he brought them I was already chewing voraciously when he told me they came from Kemal's garden, adding, apologetically, that Kemal's house with its fine terrace had been destroyed by shelling. That made me freeze up inside, belly and all.

I didn't ask about Kemal, and Omar didn't tell me. It's better that way, like Mother and Saša. I told Omar about them, about our life together before the war, but I never told him of the vacant, ruined flat or about Clarisse in the corner with her missing arm.

If you don't talk about them, then there are no questions without answers to make them not exist. Just to go away and no longer exist must be worse than the war even.

There should be an end to things, a completion. You could deal with that and grieve over it. But to be suddenly faced with a vacant silence where once was a person was impossible to deal with. It left them forever just a question mark hanging in the air, not enough even to think about.

It's like the film in school, *Hiroshima Mon Amour*. At least the girl had the sight of her dead lover to think about, knowing he had not chosen to leave her. She could grieve inwardly over that and then she got better. But the others, the ones that vanished in the bombing or turned to vapor, shadows on the wall, would always remain un-

HOTEL

finished. That gnawed at me. For myself, I don't want to be an unfinished mark in the air. I'd like there to be someone behind to care, and I don't know who that would be unless it's Clarisse, or Omar. There's Milorad, of course, but he would only feel the lack of me.

When Omar comes in he seems out of sorts.

I rush to him with a kiss, something I've never done before, always waiting for him to come to me. I kiss him again and run my fingers through his hair, stroking it. I want him to say something nice to me and then I'll smile at him. Softly he'll undress me and softly hold my breasts, stroking them and kissing them like jewels. After that I'll let him remove the rest of my clothes and he'll share my happy secret.

So I'm surprised and shocked when he only says roughly, "You'd better get undressed, hadn't you?" But I recover immediately, thinking, "When he sees me he'll be glad, and then he'll want to be gentle with me for sharing with him." So I hastily remove my clothes and fling myself back onto the mattress.

He pulls down his pants, but then he stops and says, "What's this?" I think "Now he's going to love me," but he only frowns in rejection. He seems at a loss, then he pulls up his pants and goes into the other room.

I hear him mumbling to himself and kicking things about. My open body is suddenly useless, and the smile goes out of it.

Then it occurs to me that he brought me nothing this time. It's a little thing, but it frightens me. I want to send him away to bring me back some token present, just to be sure that he would.

I hear him call distinctly from the other room. I imagine he's called out my name, "Alma!" Perhaps he's only forgotten my present.

Then he calls out again, and I'm forced to admit that what I really hear is, "Shit!"

My mind focuses on the sound and the image of that, nauseating and disgusting me. Then Alma fades away to nothing, and I feel myself warm, malleable, yielding, and putrid.

M Y BIRTHDAY IS TOMORROW. I'd almost forgotten, so I haven't told anyone yet.

It's been a year since I first came to the Sarajevo,
though it seems forever.

And it's over a month since Omar and I married ourselves in the store. True, we didn't consummate it the
first time because of my period, but after a few days
things returned to normal and he was gentle once more,
and then we did.

I don't really remember things as they were before the
war and the Sarajevo. Not exactly I mean. Oh, of course
I remember my life with Mother, then Mother and Saša;
it just seems I've been stuck on thirteen forever.

Fourteen is not old, I don't think. But I'm glad now I
didn't bring Clarisse back to the Sarajevo. Fourteen is too
big for dolls and would seem silly.

I would like to have a celebration. Mother did that
once. I don't remember which one, only a cake she baked
herself with candles on it.

I don't know who to tell. Luka would probably only
laugh, saying, "Warriors have no time for such things," or

SARAJEVO

he might say nothing at all. I could tell Milorad, but he's too little to make a party, and anyway he's sick.

Jan would make me a party, I know. Of course there'd be a cake with candles and cola and ice cream too, from Radman. I don't think they would hug me; I'm too big for that. But they might kiss me on the cheek and say, "Happy Birthday!"

When I first began meeting Omar, I was nervous and found myself holding Jan's scarf in my pocket and stroking it. That made everything okay, and I wasn't afraid at all. So I got in the habit of bringing it along. The only time I forgot was when I first got my period. I was so excited to show Omar that I left it behind. Then of course he was angry and rejected me, and I haven't forgotten the scarf since then. I'm only careful that he doesn't see it; he'd probably ask why. Usually he dozes off for a while afterwards; then I take out the scarf and run it through my hands. It smells like Jan and her perfume, and I imagine she's here. Of course if she was I'd have to return the scarf to her, but it's only right. It has my smell on it now too, that might comfort her, as hers does me.

It's so long since Jan left. But if you don't think about it, it doesn't seem long at all. It was spring when she left. Now is summer. Soon will be fall and winter. Then it starts again.

Jan belonged to the spring. Her laughter was like flowers laughing when she was here in love with Radman. Milorad's shame before the girl in the Central and the in-

HOTEL

jury to his leg were summer things. I don't know what will be a fall thing, but hope it will bring Jan back to me, and to Radman of course.

I've only seen Radman once since then. Soon after Jan left, they allowed a U.N. convoy of trucks with food and supplies to relieve Mostar. Radman went with them. I heard it was hard for them to get back out. The road was blocked, and they had to turn back many times before they were allowed to return to Sarajevo. Then one day I was on the street, just walking. There was the noise of a truck backfiring, and I looked up to see him. The armored truck was painted white with a big U.N. on the side. Radman looked tired and sad. He had a bandage around his arm that matched the white of the truck. First he didn't see me. Then he did, and his eyes brightened and he waved. I waved back, but we became less and less to each other as the truck went away. Then he was gone. My hungry stomach wished for cola and ice cream with him again. If he'd known about my birthday, I'm sure he'd have made it real. I wanted to run after him and ask him about Jan, when she would return. But I knew I'd never be able to catch the truck. All that was left of it was a little smoke from the exhaust that hung in the air.

Soon Omar will come. Now there's just myself and the mattress. When he comes, alone will go away and it will be home. There's no blood to worry about today, so everything will be okay.

We could put some boards over the front. Then we'd

SARAJEVO

have another room that's warm and dry. There'd be more freedom to move about. Sometimes, with the back room being so small, I'm constricted and I don't even want to talk.

When we lie on the mattress, my legs stick out over the end into the other room. I can feel a draft from the front windows that I don't like. It makes me feel exposed.

I wonder what Omar will bring me today.

Once a toy store had been shelled. Everyone was running and screaming, he said. Then the shelling stopped and a few people went into the store to see what they could find. A little old lady came out with a toy drum. She seemed out of place, he said, as she beat it with her hands. Then he proudly told me how brave he'd been to go into the store. That time he brought me a porcelain marionette that was a ballet dancer. Her arms and legs were attached by strings to sticks, and she danced when you flipped over the sticks. She had on a white dress and was beautiful when she danced. How I wanted to be like her! I was afraid of questions if I took her back to the Sarajevo, so I kept her here, putting her away carefully under the edge of the mattress when I didn't need her to dance for me.

I hear Omar's noise at the front of the store. I close my eyes, waiting, expecting to hear him cry out happily, "Hola!" But there's nothing, so I open them and he's standing before me with a strange look in his eyes and no words for me. There's blood on his puffed lip and a bruise under one eye. I don't know what to say. Finally, softly

HOTEL

I say, "I'm here," as though I needed an explanation or excuse.

He drops to his knees on the edge of the mattress and takes me roughly by the arms, then just holds me there, staring into my eyes like he's looking for something but doesn't know what.

I want to question him about his lip, but instead I lean back a little and lift my dress slightly to expose my thighs, as Mother did with Saša. I guess I expect him to take me in his arms, like the dead lovers. But it just seems to set him off. His face becomes contorted in its confusion: eyes and mouth, blood and bruise, all mixed together in a look of agony.

Then he cries out loudly, "There's no escape!"

Thinking he means from the city, I answer flatly, "Of course not." The guns on the hills above us will go on shelling us forever, unseen. I don't know why he can't see it, so I add, almost casually, "Things could be worse."

I don't see his hand before it slaps me.

I'm flat on my back and can see nothing but the hanging, tattered ruins of the ceiling, where I halfway expect to see Mother's stoic face appear, telling me to be quiet and make myself invisible.

My ears are full of Omar's anguished groans as his hands rip my dress up around my waist. In that instant he becomes for me those groans and those grasping, desperate hands.

I go away inside myself, and then after a while his groans subside, becoming only a series of soft little whimpers that ask my forgiveness, though his hands are still grasping and desperate.

He starts shaking and his hands lose their hold. I feel sorry for him when his sweaty head drops onto my belly, and I gently stroke his hair.

Closing my eyes, I see us as the dead lovers in the field. I wonder what they felt lying with each other, with the knowledge of each other, in the instant prior to their death. I try to imagine how that would be, really concentrating. But no matter how tight I shut my eyes, nothing comes. I can see myself laid out clean and still in a coffin as they were, but that doesn't seem like death at all. When you see them in their coffins they've already gone away, and I don't know where. It's the exact moment of dying I can't imagine. First you are, with all your memories and feelings; then there's just nothing—you've gone away, like Mother and Saša. There's nothing left but to dispose of the corpse.

While I wait for Omar to go to sleep, I reach under the mattress for my dancer. She delights me with a dance that's so fast I can't see her strings at all. But in the silence of the store I'm sure that I hear music accompanying her.

I WAIT UNTIL IT'S DARK to gently remove Omar's sleeping head and lay it aside on the mattress. Then I quietly put my dancer safely in the drawer of a cabinet before I leave Omar. At the door I look back before I go out. How peaceful he seems!

I walk quite a way without being tired. Then it's not far to the Sarajevo. The dark of the streets is an ending, something I've never liked.

As I round a corner there're some street hawkers. They've got a fire going in an oil drum to show off their stuff, spread on dirty pieces of blanket or cardboard. There're cigarettes and canned stuff, even chocolate, anything you can think of.

One has butchered pieces of "Dead Cow" that he's waving his arms over to keep the flies away. There're some buyers haggling over it, but the sight has no effect at all on my stomach. I've lost all taste for meat. I've become so accustomed to the watery rice soup, with an occasional potato, that anything else is strange. I'm sure the meat would be as tough as leather, and my teeth would refuse to chew it. It's comical to see two men and a woman actually arguing over it.

SARAJEVO

One of the men has some bills in his hand and holds them up. But the owner of the meat only laughs and says, "They're good for nothing." The other man has some canned fish he wants to trade, and that gets more interest from the seller. He weighs them in his hands, so that the money man looks anxiously at him and breaks into a sweat.

The seller appears to have made his decision by the way he's holding onto the cans.

The sad little woman keeps repeating, "I need meat for my family," as though she could actually make him see them and understand. But he only closes his hands tighter on the cans and looks right through her.

Some flies have settled on the meat since the man quit waving his arms over it.

When everything appears lost, the woman gets a desolate look in her eyes and exclaims imploringly, "I have a baby, and fresh milk."

The man's expression doesn't change. Apparently he doesn't believe her. So she hastily unbuttons her loose blouse to expose a bit of one of her swollen breasts. I'm struck at how tight it is, like a drum waiting to be played.

The man's eyes become greedy, and his hands linger on the cans, undecided. The woman draws closer to him. Her breast is right under this face, inviting him.

That does it for him. He pushes the cans back into the hands of the owner, then smiles at the woman, whose face is flooded with relief.

The can man, however, is furious at his loss, feeling

HOTEL

cheated out of what was rightly his by the sight of a swollen breast. He pulls at the woman's blouse, shouting, "Whore!" Then when she turns to him, he strikes her with a can, opening a cut on her forehead.

Her blood is accompanied by a high-pitched shriek, so loud that I wouldn't have thought her capable of making it. It sounds more like a wounded bird taking flight. Then her body becomes like a rag between the two men, as the dead cow man attempts to pull her away and the can man tries to shove her aside.

Everyone becomes involved, shouting and getting into the picture. My quietness is lost among them.

Someone in the crowd yells, "Let her have it!" I don't know if he means the meat or a beating.

Finally, between them they push the woman against some trash cans, where she collapses to the ground, sobbing over and over, "I have milk."

Meat man and can man are going at it hard, right in each other's face. I think can man wants to strike the other as he did the woman, but is put off by his size and his look.

Then a yell goes up, "Thief! Thief!" Everyone, myself included, looks around quickly to see the man with the useless handful of paper money scampering off down the street, really footing it, with the largest piece of meat cradled in his arms like a protected baby. Meat man makes a move to go after him but stops, realizing he'd have to leave the rest unprotected. His face clouds over and with his large fist he hits the can man a heavy blow

106

SARAJEVO

upside the head, knocking him to his knees. After that he wraps up the rest of his meat and moves off angrily, only pausing in passing to spit on the woman seated among the garbage.

Can man, still on his knees, cries out, "She robbed me!" Then he manages to rise, still clutching his cans, and goes to the woman, hovering over her. He doesn't spit on her but gives her a kick instead, that brings a laugh from the crowd.

Walking away alone down the street, I'm glad that I have no baby, and no breasts swollen with milk.

As I draw further away from the woman and her accusers all I can hear is the sound of my footsteps on the stones. In the silence of the streets it's as if they're first ahead of me, then behind. I can't make out if I'm following them or running away from the mechanical constancy of their *ca-plop, ca-plop, ca-plop*, like a lifeless metal robot lurching about.

I stop in front of a shop window. It's closed, but there're lights inside and I'm almost enticed into believing there's warmth and life and closeness there. Then I realize with a start that what I'm looking for and hoping to find in the mirror of the window is the reflection of myself. I want to see, really *need* to see, the face of Alma, what she's become.

But because of the brightness of the lights inside, there's nothing. Then all at once there *is* a face staring back at me only it's not mine, but that of an old man who has the sad look of tired acceptance.

HOTEL

I'm frightened by the sudden appearance of him, so that my breath is caught in my throat. Looking quickly away, I see a long, narrow shadow on the street, an extension of me, mocking me. It's not like Milorad's shadow, or poetry either. I'm overcome with the thought, "That's Alma," and all I can think of is escape.

I want to be back in my room at the Sarajevo at all costs. There I'm only a little afraid of the dark, and there are no footsteps following me.

I start walking and again I hear their sounds, becoming faster. Now there's no doubt in my mind that they're behind me, chasing me. My breath comes faster and harder and my heart pounds at my chest as I run. The only thought I recognize is, "Don't let them catch you." The shapes of the buildings are foreign and haunting to me, like something out of a movie that's not quite real.

Across the street there's a light. It's not much, only a street lamp that flashes on and off. If I can just make it to the light, then stand completely still beneath it, I know I'll be okay. I don't worry about snipers as I run, because of the dark.

Then it's over and I'm under the light. My heart is a steam locomotive working hard to climb a hill, and that's all I want, just to get to the top, without even caring what's on the other side.

The streetlight flashes off and I'm in the dark, then on and I can see myself again. I'd like to stay planted here forever with my back pasted against the hard metal of the

lamp post, like I'm trying to push myself into it. As long
as the light holds out, there'll be no shadow or footsteps to
chase me.

My mind wants to catch at anything, and it's the
thought of my birthday tomorrow. If I remain here under
the flashing of the light, maybe I'll never reach fourteen.
That seems far away right now.

What will be in fourteen? Certainly there'll be the Sar-
ajevo, with Luka and Milorad and all the rest. Of course
Omar will come to me in the store, as unyielding as ever.
I'll never be able to pry any information out of him.

Jan and Radman will return to fourteen, just as they
were in thirteen.

Of course Mother and Saša will not be there. They belong to thirteen now.

Perhaps Clarisse will still be with me, though it's possible in fourteen I'll not need her or even want her.

One thing is certain: Alma will still remain. It doesn't
make any difference whether you call her fourteen, that
sounds so big, or thirteen. She'll still be there, standing
with no reflection in store windows, and a long, narrow,
ugly shadow to contend with.

I want to make myself a poet, like Milorad, but can't,
so I remain rooted, directly under the flashing light.
When it comes, there's no shadow. That's what escape is,
not what Omar thinks. To think one could even imagine
there's anything outside Sarajevo! If you look up, all you
can see are the hills and the sky. Sometimes, when there's

HOTEL

a mist off the river, you can't tell where one lets off and the other begins.

I'd like to rise with the mist and mix with the sky. There'd be no problem getting over the hills, unless of course you were shot down before you got high enough.

The lamp goes off again, stuttering a little more than usual, complaining at having to go out. With the dark, I feel closer to the dark of Omar in the room. Perhaps only light separates us.

The way it works is you send out rays, like a smile, telling who you are, or who you think you are. Then, when they bounce off another, you get back their response, that might also be a smile, but might not.

When I gave off rays to Luka—to be wanted by him—I waited with my heart in my throat, scarcely able to breathe, until I got back silence.

When you get back silence enough times, something is lost. Then you become silence, which is what I'd become, first with Mother, then with Luka.

I know now why I wasn't afraid when the soldier took me on Zuc. It's because his wanting gave me back something besides silence, and when you've never had it before, it's almost like music. That's the way I felt with Omar at first, why I followed him home. He might as well have been playing a flute, marching resolutely down the street without even looking over his shoulder. Today, however, his silence annihilated me, and I felt like the fly beating itself against the window, hopelessly dancing to gain his attention.

SARAJEVO

It's been a long time since the light flashed. Too long. In another minute I'll stop believing in it.

Sometimes I think I'd like to be like Mother and Saša—gone away. Milorad would come to my room in the Sarajevo, opening the door after knocking, and there'd be no one there. There'd just be the absence of Alma where she was before. Then he'd just say, "Alma's gone away," putting an end to it.

My eyes have adjusted to the dark now, like I'm one with it. There's the Sarajevo, just down and across the street. Even though I can't see it clearly, the outline is unmistakable, like the shape of a familiar person waiting there for me.

If I go to it, then fall asleep on the mattress in my room, I'll be going to fourteen tomorrow.

I don't want to move. It's too hard to choose between thirteen that I know and fourteen, that's a mystery.

I'm trying to decide when there's a flash of light from the hills, then the shrill whistle that accompanies the shells.

I'm not worried that it's coming to claim me. Once you hear the whistle you're already out of danger. It's just in the time between the light and the whistle that you have to hold your breath. It's not long enough to bother you. But in that brief instant you stop, waiting to see if you'll continue or not.

I can see the Sarajevo lit up for an instant. It beckons to me, and I run to it.

THE FLASHES AND THE WHISTLES have stopped.
There's Mira's kiosk before the hotel, standing sentinel.

The door is open. It's really only a board she's placed over the knocked-out entrance. Still, it's always in place whether she's at home or not. She's very careful about that, so it's strange to see it open.

It's quiet, and too dark to see inside. I want to call out "Mira!" but then I remember the coldness of her hand the time she wanted to draw me inside.

I'd like to just skip on past into the Sarajevo, but the open door won't let me. It's funny how little things can make a difference. Just the absence of that rough piece of board in the doorway makes it seem as though the round little cubicle she calls home has been violated.

I go around the kiosk carefully, then when I return to the opening, it's still there calling to me. So now I do call out, "Mira," only quietly, while knocking at the same time.

Nothing. That's not satisfactory, so I call and knock again. She's very private with her grief and her pain, and I don't want to disturb her.

SARAJEVO

Then there's a sound, like when a doctor listens to your chest with his cold stethoscope and tells you to breathe out as hard as you can.

Now I've got an excuse to go inside. If I'm caught, I can say I heard the noise and went to investigate. I've always wondered how she could live there, in a space so small.

There's hardly any room to stand, but what strikes me first of all is how warm and safe it feels, like you were inside a cocoon. Even though it's a flimsy construction, I feel safe from the shells, so I collapse happily, like Clarisse when I drop her on the bed. It's like when I was very small and I'd run laughing to burrow under the bedcovers to hide from Father, still laughing to make it easy for him to find me there.

But the sound of my laughter is strange now, like it belongs to someone else.

I stretch out my legs, which is nearly impossible in the close quarters, and they touch another pair of legs that are very still and quiet. It's like bumping into Clarisse in the bed at night.

I hear my voice say, "Excuse me, please."

As soon as I've said it, though, I realize there's no need.

I've been sitting with Mira a long time, just talking to her. I leaned her up against the wall so she could hear me better. I didn't have to shut her eyes for her. She shut them before she went away.

I told her about Omar and our room in the store, how we've made a life together there, thinking that's what she'd like to hear most. She's a good listener, never once interrupting.

I even told her how proud I'd been to get my period. I wanted to share it with someone anyway. She seems pleased in a way that I chose her. There's something like a smile on her face.

I wonder what to talk about next, not wanting to run on, but a little afraid to be quiet with her. So I tell her how nice she looks, then ask her about herself, starting with her home. I want to know what her life was like before, if she's ever had any of the same feelings I've had, like hating my plainness, or wanting for Luka or Omar to love me.

Then I think perhaps she'd like to hear about my life before, so I start rattling it off, telling her everything. I'm surprised to find how much we have in common. When I get to the part about Mother going away, I hesitate, worrying that it might hurt her feelings that Mother had Saša to go away with, and she'd had no one. But then I think, "I'm here," and say it out loud. After that I feel better for her.

When I get tired of talking I don't know what else to do, so I smooth her hair back from her face. I'm surprised at its baby softness. You'd never have guessed it from looking at her. She must have been very proud of it and brushed it in private to keep it that way. It was her little secret, but now I've found it out, making us closer.

I wish I had something to wipe the blood away from her face. There's a big glob on her forehead right at the hairline. Another streak's run down all the way to her chin.

SARAJEVO

It's dried, though, and hard to remove. I try spitting on my sleeve, then rubbing hard at it, but I don't have enough spit to do a good job, only smearing it and making it worse.

I don't know what happened to her. She has some bruises and a cut on her arm. It looks as though someone threw stones at her. It must have been somewhere else, because there's no damage to her house. Her door is very carefully laid up against the inside of the kiosk, like she just popped in for a minute and planned to go right out again.

I'm surprised she could drag herself this far. I know no one from the Sarajevo would do this to her, even though they made fun of her. Once I heard that the men of the neighborhood found out she'd sold herself to some soldiers for candy and cigarettes. Then they beat her, but they couldn't make her cry. She just sat there and looked at them until they got tired and went away. When I heard about it I thought that they were jealous over the candy and cigarettes and beat her because they had nothing to sell. The story went that, at the last, before they left her, one hit her square on the nose, breaking it. Then he looked at her misshapen face and mocked, "Now you'll have nothing to sell." The housewife that I heard telling it seemed pleased when she came to that part.

Perhaps they came back, not content with merely beating her. Her presence here has always made people uneasy, even myself at times. I feel bad about that now, wishing I could change it.

I get an idea, sitting up straight next to her and putting

115

an arm around her shoulders. I want to tell her about the dead lovers. Not about how they were in the field, abused and alone, but how they were honored in the sanctuary: how quiet and respectful all their visitors were, how Omar and I succeeded in reuniting them.

My voice becomes lower and soothing while I tell her about it. And when I've finished, I know she's pleased. Now she doesn't have to be afraid at going away. Everyone needs something warm and pleasant to hold onto when going away, even if it's only an idea or a story.

I don't want to leave her, but I have to go. They'll lock the door to the Sarajevo if it gets too late. Then I'll have to beat on it, making a racket that will require explanations that I don't have just now.

I'm talked out, but glad that I was here for her. The only bad thing was the sound of her breath going out as I stood outside earlier. That must have been her last, and there was no one here to catch it. But then I remember saying her name out loud just before. She must have heard that. I hope she did anyway.

I don't want to say good-bye to her, so I fumble around with my words, finally blurting out, "Tomorrow is my birthday!" That sounds silly, but she doesn't mind, I don't think.

As I start to go, there's the buzzing of a fly around the blood on her face. It makes me *furious!* that she can't do anything, but just has to sit there. Swiftly I clap my hands together over the fly and put an end to its buzzing mockery.

SARAJEVO

Then, reaching into my blouse, I take out Jan's scarf, feeling its pleasant silkiness. I put it in Mira's hands and close them over it in her lap.

Being in the open again makes me shiver. On the sidewalk between Mira's kiosk and the Sarajevo are the ruins of our two bicycles. A truck backed over them one day. Luka was furious, and you could feel some of his power leaving him. Now they seem like two of the frozen figures from Pompeii that I saw on slides in school. The crushed seats are the crying faces, and the handlebars are arms flung wide, imploring.

Then I see Milorad. Waiting for me on the steps of the Sarajevo, he looks even smaller than usual.

His eyes find mine and, looking for sympathy, he says, "My leg hurts." But I'm drained and have none left to give him. If I had any, I'd use it on myself.

"Go to bed," is all I say, brushing past him on my way inside.

Later in my room, I lie on the mattress and stare quietly into the dark until I'm sure it must be past midnight. Then I turn on my side and close my eyes.

It's my birthday.

I'm fourteen, at last.

W E'RE ALMOST AT THE EDGE of the gardens. We've left the Miljacka behind, and now we're climbing away from it out of the fog to the edge of the plain. It's the 500th day; I heard someone say so. There're only ten of us. Luka said that was enough for the job.

It's strange coming out of the mist. Ilija has a big smile, looking like he wants to sing. Dejan is moody as always. Milorad has a pained expression, trying hard to keep up, sometimes dragging the leg. Nenad is only silent.

I hold my breath when it's time for Luka to appear out of the fog. He is our glue. Without him will the Sarajevo be there when we get back?

It was Ilija's idea to raid the gardens. I think he meant it as a joke because he laughed when he said it. Luka, however, took it up instantly. Then Ilija was amazed at his genius in thinking of it. That was last night. Luka said we would go right away, in the morning. By the time we turned in, the whole thing had become his project.

This morning before we left, Luka looked like a gargoyle as he perched on his trash can throne, stone-faced, with his chin in his hand, like he was guarding the Sarajevo and warding off evil spirits. When I saw him like the old Luka, I wanted to run to him and kiss his hands. But then he turned his face to me with a look that was vacant. I knew it wasn't drugs. I don't think they concern him anymore. The war has become his drug.

We all went to Sandra's room this morning before we left. She's been coughing a lot. She was in the rain and got wet, and that night she was shivering and feverish. We put her to bed and kept her warm, but she hasn't gotten any better.

While we were gathered around her bed before leaving for the gardens, Sandra looked at us with her big eyes, then tried to get up. Luka said nothing, oblivious to her effort, leaving it up to her own strength. Milorad turned pale as he watched Sandra's effort and saw Luka's look, which had already dismissed her, like she was a wounded animal left behind as a sacrifice. I couldn't stand her torment, so finally I put my hand on her shoulder and gently pushed her back down. That made her eyes happy.

Luka said we will eat like kings. That made everyone happy, except maybe Sandra and Milorad. Her eyes stayed the same when Luka told her about the raid on the gardens. She tried to smile a little encouragement to him, but was too weak. Then she had a coughing fit from the effort. I raised her head and held a towel under her chin for her to spit in. There was blood in it. Milorad broke down and told Luka we should take her to see a doctor at the hospital. But Luka only snorted angrily and said, "No doctors! See what happened to Adnan?"

Milorad fell silent. Adnan never came back to us. The

stumps of legs developed an infection that spread, and then he'd gone away. We never saw him again after the visit to the hospital to take him the toy gun. So that's the way I remember him, laughing and shooting the gun *pow!* at imaginary enemies.

Later Luka went alone to the hospital to fetch Adnan's few belongings. There was no one else to go. Adnan was orphaned early on by the war, and we were all he had.

We all waited silently for Luka on the steps of the Sarajevo. When he came down the street with Adnan's little bundle in his arms, Milorad ran to him, looking like he wanted to cry. Luka's lips only moved a little and said nothing, but his eyes dropped to Adnan's bundle, the toy gun sticking out of it like a flag.

After a painful silence Milorad asked plaintively, "Where is Adnan? What have they done to him?"

That made Luka mad. He smiled almost meanly and pulled the gun from the bundle, handing it to Milorad in such a way that he couldn't refuse it.

"You'll take his place," Luka said. Then he went inside, leaving us alone on the steps.

I watched a spider working busily at making a web, as if the war didn't bother it at all. Then I looked up to see Milorad pacing up and down, the gun on his shoulder as he smiled broadly. I asked him what he was doing and he replied proudly, "I'm on guard." He wheeled around and went the other way. Looking at the back of him, I was sad.

That night it took us a long time to get a fire going. The only pieces of wood we had had gotten wet. Luka got up

SARAJEVO

and went inside. He came back and threw something in the fire. I couldn't quite make out what because of the shadows. But then the fire blazed up, looking like one of the rockets, and I saw it was a pair of Adnan's pants that Luka had thrown on it. I knew they were Adnan's because they'd been cut off at the knees to fit his stubs.

They made a queer smell as they burned. I looked at Luka's face. He was staring into the flames, unaware of me. I wondered what he saw there.

It's strange. When the raid was proposed, then settled on by Luka, no one noticed the fact that we'd be taking food from others just like ourselves, and perhaps as hungry. If they did, they didn't say so. There was nothing of regret or indecision in their faces, only happiness at the thought of a full stomach. We in the Sarajevo have always been scavengers, that's true. But before it was strictly anonymous, from ruined houses and stores. Everyone did that. Stealing from the Centrals was alright because Luka's force made them enemies. Besides, other than the one raid that was botched because of the incident of Milorad and the girl, my hands have never been involved. I've only eaten the others' stealing, without thinking about it. I'm sure that before I'd never have even considered stealing from the gardens, which have always been off-limits and respected by all.

But now I don't know. I'm here with them anyway. It's the 500th day, as I've said, and we're all hungry, my stomach no less than theirs.

121

HOTEL

Mira never stole food. At least I don't think so. Maybe it's true, like they said, that she sold herself, but that's not the same as stealing. I don't know which would be worse, though I think I'd rather steal than sell myself. But then, Mira never made the 500th day. It was last month that she went away.

I didn't go out to watch as grownups from the neighborhood took her away. I'd already said good-bye to her and, anyway, I could hear the hammer blows—like final insults flung at her—as they boarded up her kiosk.

Later that afternoon I went out onto the quiet street. I asked a man what had become of her. He just stood there looking lost with nothing to do, his hands in his pockets.

Finally, emotionless, he said, "They took her away and buried her, like the rest."

That didn't satisfy me, so I asked where. They'd put her in a mass grave toward the edge of the city. They hadn't thought that she belonged in an individual grave in the field next to the ruins of Zetra stadium because she wasn't from Sarajevo and had left no relatives behind. It bothered me that she was so far from her kiosk, but I was glad to learn they'd made a little wooden coffin for her, so she'd feel at home.

Perhaps it was different after the 500th day, like a mark was drawn, and people and things changed afterwards. In a way Mira was lucky to have gotten away.

Patches of fog are beginning to break apart and lift off the Miljacka. It will be light soon.

SARAJEVO

"The fog is our great protector," I've heard many say. The Miljacka gives it to us to protect us from the sniper fire from the hills. But though it helps to keep the bullets out, it also hems us in. We're free to move around within it, but can't break free. Our freedom is also our cage.

In the rapidly becoming light I can see the spire of the Imperial Mosque rising toward heaven. Beside the mosque there's a very old graveyard, whose tilted, turbanlike headstones also point heavenwards, imploringly. The gardens are just outside, along the stone wall of the cemetery.

I asked Milorad once about being Muslim, and he told me a few things, just enough to confuse me. Once Saša and some men were talking about Muslims. Saša's face clouded up and he spit on the ground. "They're unbelievers," he said. But I don't understand why Milorad's god should be hated just because he has a different name.

Right in the middle of the siege, our Pop gave a magnificent talk. They were not right, he said, but neither were we to oppose violence with violence, making both wrong. God would decide in the end and punish the wicked and the offenders. He sounded very convinced of it all, and everyone agreed with him, shaking his hand and congratulating him.

A few months later his wife, the Popadja, was coming home through the streets carrying some loaves of bread when she was taken away by a mortar shell. It must have been a big one because I heard it whispered that "there was nothing left of her to bury."

HOTEL

The next week we all went to church. Everyone wanted to see how the Pop would hold up.

He started off okay, but then during the sermon there was the sound of a shell exploding. Even though it was not close, he closed his eyes for a moment. When he opened them, there was a tear running down his cheek as he said, "I'm sorry, but I cannot believe in a God who permits such things to happen." Then he closed his book and went out through the side entrance behind the altar.

Everyone walked out in silence, feeling a little disappointed. I heard a man say, "He's weak. He's lost his faith." But perhaps he was weak before, and only became strong when he admitted his weakness.

Everything is quiet. The fog risen off the Miljacka follows us like ghosts, rapid, pursuing. We are invisible but for the red knapsacks we carry to haul away our thefts.

Milorad's in constant pain. I took a look at his leg last night, holding him down to do it. It's all reddish around the cut. I think it's infected. There was some pus coming out of it that I didn't like the look of. So I wiped it away with a piece of rag, trying to be careful. Even so he winced, but when I asked him, "Did I hurt you?" he only shook his head manfully. Ever since they praised him over his wound he's lost his innocence. Now he feels he has to live up to their standards. I liked him better as he was before.

I look at the others' faces and think, "We're quiet because we feel our shame," but I don't know if that's true.

SARAJEVO

I don't even want to think about it, so I shake my head and take a deep breath of the morning air. It seems like any other morning with its smell of flowers that we can't yet see.

But this is not just any morning. With the fog around us I could pretend. As it goes away, I can feel the pretend going out of me. It doesn't go away all of a sudden, like being hit in the stomach, but gradually, like exhaling slowly on a cold morning. When you lose pretend your stomach gets all scared inside, making sounds like you're hungry. Then you'll do anything to make sure you exist.

That's why I think Mira really sold herself to the soldiers, not because of hunger, but because she needed another's touch to make her still be real. Sometimes I get that way myself. Then pinching myself doesn't do. But when I wait for Omar I begin to feel real. When he's there and needs me it's even better. I'm warm and secure inside until he's gone. Even then it lasts a while, with the smell of him lingering there with me.

At the edge of the gardens the air is heavy with the smell of turned earth that's been wet by the fog. Luka is first and holds up his hand at the frail barricade, only odd pieces of wood held together by wire. It's certainly not capable of keeping anyone out. The equally fragile gate is held closed only by a piece of rope looped over a post.

For myself, I've never understood about fences. There're so many of them. I never really noticed before the war. Now they're everywhere. If you think about it, they're rather silly.

HOTEL

If I had it to decide, I'd never build a fence. It must be a lot of trouble to build them, then maintain them, not to mention keeping them locked, even guarding them, like the barbed-wire fences Radman and the U.N. soldiers put up around themselves. Maybe they feel more secure, like I do in the Sarajevo or in the store with Omar. Even though I know a mortar shell could reach me there, I never think about it after I enter and close the door behind me. Then I actually feel safe, like nothing can touch me.

Perhaps that's why fences got started. There's the need to put up something around us to keep the others out. Still, it seems a shame.

The fog has finally left us completely exposed, trapped in the middle of a war between the river and the hills, where escape has no meaning.

LUKA OPENS THE GATE AND goes through the fence. Then all the others rush through, Milorad and myself last of all. Milorad stumbles a little on his bad leg, and he looks up at me with his sad eyes. I try to give him a smile, but it doesn't quite come off. There's no one else about. It's early yet. Soon the gardeners will come to their plots, that are marked off only by lines drawn in the earth. Though the gardens have been here almost from the start of the siege, Mother never showed any interest in them. She had Saša then, so she felt it was beneath her.

Dejan pulls a ripe squash. He laughs and tosses it across to Ilija, shouting, "Catch!" But Ilija is too late; the squash hits him in the chest with a thud, then falls to the ground as he fumbles after it. First he's angry; then he grabs the squash and flings it at Milorad. When Milorad catches it he laughs too. Then he throws the squash and they all break out into laughter, running and throwing.

Luka stands aside solemnly, letting it go on for a while. Nenad is there with him. I don't think his wall of silence could ever break down and let him join in.

In their haste to enjoy themselves they're stomping

over some of the plants—beets, squash, and cabbage.
Ilija runs to the edge of a plot that's marked by a narrow
line of bare earth, then hides from Milorad behind some
corn stalks. He can't keep still, however. The stalks begin
waving like they're alive. When Milorad comes close, the
corn laughs as Ilija breaks down behind his shield. Milorad parts some of the stalks, then dives into them, shouting, "I've got you now!" But Ilija skips away, still laughing. Milorad trips and falls flat on his face. The corn
stalks seem to yell, "Ow!" Milorad gets up with mud on
his face and the beginning of a smile; then he grimaces
because he's hurt his leg again.

Luka whistles, shrill and piercing, to call them to attention, and they rush to his side like toy soldiers waiting
for a command. He sends Ilija after corn, Dejan after cabbage. After they pick their helpers, Milorad is left standing expectantly, wiping at the mud on his face with the
ragged tail of his shirt. I'm off to the side, watching, not
wanting to know if I'm to be a part of it or not.

Luka puts a hand on Milorad's shoulder, telling him,
"You're in charge of carrots. Don't fail me." Before he lets
Milorad go, he turns to look flatly at me, and I know I'm
to be his helper. I don't know how that makes me feel,
preferring not to think of it, so when Milorad calls,
"Coming, Alma?" I blindly follow.

We start to pull up the carrots, dusting them off before
putting them in our knapsacks. We got the bright red
sacks when a department store was shelled and we happened to be close by.

SARAJEVO

Dejan and Ilija start to race one another, running and trying to see who can fill their sack first. Milorad takes it up and they really go at it, making quite a racket until Luka tells them to be quiet. He leans on the fence, taking everything in, but not a part of it.

I won't race them, just working steadily at the carrots. Before I know it, I've left them a little behind, having pulled my way over near the stone fence. I can hear their muffled voices through the plants.

Working hard, I'm right up to the stone fence with the cemetery on the other side. The stone is cool and inviting as I run my hand along its smoothness. A sudden wave of release washes over me, and I close my eyes to enjoy it, as I do sometimes in the room with Omar. I almost forget where I am, thinking maybe I'm a child again, until my hand comes to a jagged edge that rakes across it in pain. I open my eyes with a start, but I'm more annoyed than hurt. I eye the fence fiercely and would like to punish it for taking my dream away. Instead, I do the next best thing, falling down to rest and nuzzling up against the cool, hard, unmoving stone that supports my tired back.

I didn't know I was tired before, but now I ache all over with it. I take a carrot from my knapsack, on the ground between my legs. I hear Milorad call, "Alma!" off to the right, but I don't answer. He's too far away, and I don't want to be bothered. I take a bite of carrot, brushing it off first, and I like the taste of it. No one will know.

The remnants of the hiding fog are rising fast out of the valley now, like hurrying patches of clouds. We'll have to hurry with them. Soon it will be fully light. Then the gardeners will come, and we'll have to be gone. I'm not worried about sitting here resting. Even if Luka or one of the others discovers me, they can't criticize me. My sack is already full. If they start to say anything, I'll merely open the sack and show them, then they'll have to shut up. In fact, I'd almost like to be discovered so I could do it.

Dejan's and Ilija's heads pop up and down as they pick. They resemble little stick figures in a shooting gallery. Sometimes on the streets in Sarajevo, the people look that way too. They're stiff and awkward, like puppets on strings. Their eyes dart here and there like little machines. If you could peel off their skin, you'd probably find springs and gears inside.

Even Omar's eyes have become that way, where they weren't before. However, they lose some of it when we're together in the room, softening a little. Then when it's time to go, they become hard and suspicious again—that I don't care to see.

Luka's eyes are never scared and darting, but always flat. When I first came to the Sarajevo, his were laughing eyes, but that's gone away and there's nothing to replace it. Maybe for him there is nothing. He's a product of the war; without it, he would never have been a chief.

I no longer go to his room and lie on his mattress waiting for him in pretend, as I used to. Partly it's because of Omar, but mostly because I know there's no use.

It's good to be in the gardens, though I'm tired of watching the others at their games. Sometimes I think it's all only a game. If I stopped in the street, clapped my hands loudly, and called, "Time!" they would all stop and put down their guns. The game would be over, and there'd be no winners, but everyone would be friends and smiles and happiness. We'd all shake hands and hug one another, not looking to see who we were hugging. And the Sarajevo would be big enough for everyone to fit into. We'd have a feast in the courtyard with baklava and ice cream and ručak, toasting one another. Then we'd troop off to the hospital and no one would be there; no patients, I mean, just doctors and nurses, who'd greet us smiling. And I'd go fetch Clarisse again, and find Mother and Saša. I don't know what I'd do about Omar and Luka, but I'd work something out. We'd all be happy, except, I guess, those who had gone away and couldn't be happy anymore . . .

"What are you clapping for?" I open my eyes to find Milorad in my face, peering down at me in my embarrassment. I don't want to answer him, wishing he'd just go away. So I pull a carrot from my sack and hand it to him. That satisfies him, as almost any kind of attention will. He sits down close to me, holding his bad leg and grimacing. He looks so funny with his face all screwed up and the carrot sticking out of his mouth, that I have to laugh.

"What are you laughing at?"

"You, silly. You're a silly goose." His questions annoy me. Everything must be explained to him. Some things are not to be explained; they just are. I'm old enough to know that. That's why I never ask too many questions, not out loud anyway. Or maybe I got it from Mother, I don't know.

"Imgowintobeacheefsumday." I can't understand a thing he says with his mouth full, except at the end I think I catch, "Sunday." Then I realize I don't know what day it is, as if that could have a meaning anyway. Normally, I guess, people get some expectation of things by the ordering together of days, weeks, and months, their regular coming and going. That's so you can give a time to a thing, looking forward to it happening, as, "We'll go to church on Sunday," or, "School will be over next month." That way the mind could think of them in advance and get prepared. Some things, like going away, never get a time attached to them, at least not in advance. It's always past tense, like "Mira went away last month," only now last month has lost all meaning. I hate to think of Mira like that, or Mother and Saša, and can't imagine myself dissolving and fading away.

It doesn't matter if today is a Sunday or Monday or Tuesday. It's the 500th day, that's all that counts, and I'm not really sure what that means except as a mark between enduring yesterday and enduring tomorrow. Suddenly I laugh for no reason at all.

Milorad must think I'm laughing at him, because he takes the carrot out of his mouth and repeats himself more clearly, "I'm going to be a chief someday," as though the repetition will make it so. But really, even hearing it clearly, "someday" has no more meaning to me than "Sunday"; my mind just can't focus on it long enough to make it exist.

Milorad makes his thumb and forefinger into a gun, extending it toward Dejan and Ilija. Then he shoots them with, "*Pow! Pow!*"

"Stop it!" I'm angry as I slap his arm down.

He doesn't seem to give it a thought, however, putting the carrot back in his mouth like a giant pacifier. He hands me one too, then pulls himself up to look over the low stone wall.

"Somanycrosses." I know what he said this time, even without him repeating it. The carrot tastes good, the hardness making me think of chewing and nothing else.

"Why so many?" he asks.

I don't know what to answer. Has the fact of the war somehow passed him by, except for his leg, which he can't ignore? Jumping up, I'd like to snatch him off the wall. It's as though his question negates Mira and Adnan and all the others. But seeing the smallness and defenselessness of his back, I lose my anger and join him leaning over the wall.

It's startling. Not what I thought at all. Now I understand his question. There're crosses *everywhere*. Intermixed with the stone ones, that have a dignity about them because of their permanence, are rows of makeshift wooden ones. Some are quite elaborate with the names carved, others no more than two sticks tied together, nameless.

Those scare me. I don't want to look at them, but must.

HOTEL

They demand my attention, as if they need to make up for the fact that they have no names. One, that is just two jagged pieces of board, is held together by a bright yellow scarf bound tightly around them. There's something anguished about the hopelessness of the knot. It reminds me of Jan's scarf, and I reach for it where it should be in my blouse. Then I recall that I gave it to Mira to go away with. I wonder if they used it to bind up her cross. She could be there somewhere among them now, resting.

"Why so many?"

I'm glad for Milorad's question now, even the repetition of it, as it allows me to look away from the crosses to the isolation of his face, only to discover there's not much difference between them.

My lips start to answer him, though I don't know what they'll say.

Then there's a low whistle. At first I think it's Luka, and turn in his direction. Dejan and Ilija are standing straight. Ilija has dropped his knapsack. Its red looks strangely out of place, like a pool of blood against the bare earth. Dejan is holding his before him like a shield. Luka too is standing straight and stiff. They all have their heads turned away, toward the Miljacka and the hills beyond, as though they're looking at someone approaching. Then there's the whistle again, louder. I know it's not Luka; his lips didn't move. Then Luka yells something I can't make out, and the others run toward him.

The shelling's started again.

SARAJEVO

Milorad and I remain momentarily frozen. Then I grab his shirt and pull him back from the wall so suddenly that he yells, "What?"

I don't have time to answer. The whistling becomes shrill and nearer, taking my breath away. Then it ends with a *bang!* down the hill between the river and the gardens. There are other whistles, but they are going away from us, leaving us alone.

It was not for us that they came this time. We can breathe again.

We start to run, only Milorad's forgotten his sack of carrots and has to go back for it. He'd rather face the whistles than the sight of Luka's disapproving eyes.

We run together hand in hand. We're together with the others going out the gate, which remains hanging open like good-bye.

We go back down the hill much faster than we came up, even though the whistles are far away and defeated now. Milorad drops my hand disdainfully, remembering he's too big for hands.

Then we stop. Our breaths are all together in a circle, coming fast. Luka must have run too, because he's with us now. Ilija laughs with relief. We can hardly hear the whistles at all; perhaps we imagined them.

We all remember we're hungry at once. Ilija reaches into my sack for a carrot and takes a big bite of it, not even bothering to brush it off. It makes a noise *crunch!* that seems to echo across the hill. Milorad takes two carrots

HOTEL

and shoves one at me. I notice that it's slightly sweet, as I watch the others' faces. How young they seem, that I've never seen before.

We start off down the hill again, single file because of the path. The river's very clear below us. Milorad's directly in front of me. The back of his head is laughing as he bounces up and down, pleased now that he came.

I'm chewing on the carrot, savoring it. It's not baklava, but it's better than nothing. It's good to be together, following Luka again. It was a good tiredness from picking in the gardens and watching the others racing one another. Now that it's over, it was even good losing our breaths running from the whistles. I don't think about the crosses in the cemetery.

Up ahead there must be a bend in the trail because our line turns. We're in an open place. Then the line stops, so quickly that I run into Milorad's back, making him cry out.

Playfully, I'm about to start in at him with, "Milorad is a 'fraidy cat!" but then he moves aside, back toward me for comfort, and I see why the line stopped and who the whistles came for.

They're lying on the ground, not holding one another—I guess there wasn't time for that—but near one another. I'm glad for that. There're two of them, one older than the other. One looks like a mother and the other a daughter. The mother is lying face down as though she doesn't want to see. Her arms are spread out from her, as if she was begging for mercy when it happened. She'd been carrying two plastic jugs of water from the river to take to her plants in the garden. The daughter's face is staring straight up at us, asking us why. Or maybe she's looking past us to the sky. It's not certain either way.

Milorad turns his face to me. I'm afraid he's going to ask for an explanation again. But he keeps quiet. At first I'm relieved at his quiet, but then I want to scream over and over from the hillside until the quiet goes away. Quiet is acceptance, and I don't feel accepting.

We stopped so quickly, everything happened so fast, that my mouth is still full of carrot. Now, looking at them, mother and daughter, I understand that perhaps it was carrots they came for. Then I'm certain of it. This carrot brought them here to the hill to meet the whistles. With it, I'm chewing the life out of them. I can't swallow. Just the presence of it in my mouth is choking me.

I can't take my eyes off them, especially the daughter. Her face is like that of a sister.

Milorad is still looking at me. I'd like to yell at him to go away and leave me alone. His gaze seems to blame me for taking the carrot from them.

I hear Ilija's voice, guilty and uncertain, asking, "What will we do?" and with no hesitation, Luka's answering, "Nothing."

The chewed piece of carrot is going to explode in my mouth and come out my nose. I can feel it beginning. But just when I think that I'll have to spit it out or burst our line starts moving again down the hill. With a guilty relief and an easing in my stomach, I'm finally able to tear my eyes away from those of the daughter.

I wait until we've put a little distance between us and them. Then, dropping back and turning my head aside so the others can't see, I quickly spit out the torturing carrot as far as I can. I wipe my mouth with the back of my hand, hoping the taste will go away, but it stays there. I'm tormented by it until we reach the river. Pretending I'm thirsty, I leave the others and run down to the edge to try to wash it out of me.

When I join the line again, thankfully Milorad doesn't look back. Their backs are obscene marching steadily away, stronger because of the food. I'm sure my back must carry the same obscenity. I can't see it, but I can feel the weight of it.

I can forgive, or at least allow, for Luka's "Nothing," even the flatness of his tone. What I can't overlook is his lack of hesitation in delivering it. If nothing else the mother and daughter deserved that from us, the thieves of their carrots, at least a brief hesitation in pronouncing them nothing.

I can't look at Luka, so I keep my eyes on Milorad, even though his limp gives the impression that we're slinking away. I'd like to look down at the ground, but don't. Watching his limp, I accept the guilt, and the ugliness and nausea attached to it, as a penance.

I don't think I'll eat carrots again, ever.

I DON'T KNOW THE EXACT ending of summer—the date, I mean—but I can sense the beginning of it. The days are getting shorter. It's funny that endings in nature have beginnings that continue for a while, lessening before they end, whereas endings in your life just go *kaplunk!* and finish themselves right away, like Mi a, or Mother and Saša going away. I think it would be easier if you could see a beginning to an end and then prepare yourself, getting a grip on it to be able to hold yourself in. I don't know what would be the beginning of the end of Mira, certainly not of Mother and Saša. Maybe unless you saw the beginning of the end right away, it was too late once you were in it.

Omar is gone, perhaps like the rest, though I saw him go. I don't know if he'll come back. A little while ago the cold back of him said good-bye. The empty chill of the ruined store closed over the space where he had been, and for a moment, like drawing a breath, I wondered if he had ever been. Perhaps I imagined him. Perhaps when I was in the sanctuary of the dead lovers my mind created the need for an Omar, and I just invented him, and then all the rest.

HOTEL

Perhaps I'm still there in the sanctuary, and everything that's happened between then and now is only a dream. Maybe I'm hypnotized by the sight of them lying so quietly in the dim, flickering candlelight. In a minute I'll wake up, blinking my eyes to clear them. I'll recognize the lie of it all, smiling at my inventiveness, thinking, "What a clever girl, Alma!" Then I'll rush outside through the heavy doors and be on my way back to the Sarajevo and Luka, who's undoubtedly missed me.

No. Omar is real, as real as I am. I know because the poster on the wall is still there, only it's staring now, not smiling. It's still lopsided, however. The tape I used to tack it up was old and one corner slipped.

It's a travel poster of a ship, with palm trees on an island. The ship is headed to the trees and the island rather than away. I like that. Big bright blue letters on the poster say, "Pleasure Island," and I like that too.

There used to be a travel agency down the street. The front is ruined like our store, and the people who worked there have gone away. But the poster was still there when I passed on my way here today. It looked very proud to be in the window, proclaiming happily, "Pleasure Island." It gave me the feeling that if I just went inside the travel shop, I would be there, without the need of a ship even. I tried to imagine what it would be like, the sun and the water and the palms. But try as hard as I might, I couldn't see myself among them. So I went into the shop, took down the poster, rolled it up, and brought it back here so it could be proud and happy on our wall. I know the people of the agency wouldn't mind. They'd probably be glad someone happened along and found some use for it.

When I first brought it home, it made me happy. I thought if I came often and stared at it very hard, really concentrating, the ship would come right out of the poster into the room, with its noises and colors and smells, ready for me to board. Either that, or I'd be able to go into the poster, which would be even better. When I'd learned how to go there, I'd teach Omar and he could go with me. We'd be able to leave Sarajevo anytime we wanted. It would be our escape.

I began to wonder about the ship and who was on it. Would it just be vacationers, laughing and carefree and spending their money? Or is it possible Mother and Saša and the others had seen the poster and gone into it? Maybe Omar himself was going there now, without telling me. That's probably why he didn't look back; he felt guilty at leaving me behind. It's certain he must have seen the poster. He undoubtedly recognized where it could take him even before I did. Mother would never have thought of it, I'm sure, but Saša might have.

If I went on the ship, even with Omar, I'd be sad to leave the others in the Sarajevo behind. I don't think I'd be able to enjoy the sun and the water and the palms knowing they were left behind. On the ship, I'm sure I'd wonder about them—what they were doing at various times of the day, about Milorad's leg and Sandra's cough, if the courtyard with its sycamore remained the same, or if the war finally came to visit there.

HOTEL

It's funny; I'm not at all jealous of Sandra anymore. As soon as she got sick I stopped thinking of her as the Princess Sandra. Her face lost its radiance and innocence with the fever and became just the face of fear and resignation, which is all too familiar to me.

Luka wrote her off right away, at least with his look. I don't know if he even gave it a thought. I know it would be the same if I became sick, and that leaves me cold. Sometimes I wonder how it is that I ever loved him.

That makes me think of Jan. She's been away from Radman a long time, all through the summer. If she'd been here to see him pass on the truck that day, with his tired, sad eyes and his bandaged arm, I wonder if she would still have loved him.

He's a different Radman now from the smiling, laughing Radman of the spring, just as Luka is no longer the yelling, triumphant Luka returning from a raid on the Centrals. They've both become like the ruined jukebox in the lobby—once capable of playing music, but now just a silent, empty shell.

I wonder where laughter goes when it disappears from your eyes. I don't wonder about mine so much because, growing up with Mother, they never learned to laugh much in the first place. The war was not so much a change as an extension of her silence, with the whistling of the shells and the sight of burning people thrown in. When they finish whistling or burning, they become merely silences also. That's what makes you able to stand them. If you only wait long enough, there's silence in the

SARAJEVO

end. Then you get a chance to catch your breath before the next comes along.

When Sandra finishes coughing, she will become silence. I don't like to think about it, but part of me will be relieved not to hear her anymore. Perhaps it will also be a relief for her. When I go to her to put a wet rag on her forehead, her eyes are apologetic for the sounds she makes.

Once she looked up at me with her big eyes, and for an instant I saw there the same ignorant innocence of it all she had in the beginning. Suddenly sick, I wanted to run out of the room, down the stairs, then down the street until I could run no more and she was forgotten. But before I could move she grabbed my hand, pulling it close to her with a strength I didn't know she had. Her eyes became calm with an acceptance that was not ignorance, and I knew why I'd wanted to run.

Without realizing it, I'd always taken comfort in her ignorance. She was unseeing for all of us, and we could hide behind her eyes, taking refuge there, like in the protection of the courtyard.

Now that she's lost it, we're forced to face the reality of a handful of cold rice in an empty stomach, or carrying water all the way from the river, or stealing food from the Miljacka gardens. Without her unknowing eyes to look through, we can no longer pretend the rockets are fireworks, but must admit that their whistling is a voice that screams, "I'm coming to take you away!" Now I know that many times, even as we sat in the courtyard listening, it

HOTEL

would have been a secret relief if one of them had come for me.

Maybe that's the way Omar feels now. Maybe he went away to look for the source of the whistling and to find his relief there. Acceptance can be relief once you've completely assimilated it, as Sandra has.

The last thing Omar said to me was, "I'm just going out for a walk." I didn't question him about it, even though his eyes said something different. They told me what his voice did not want to, about going away, and perhaps not coming back.

It's not because of me he went away.

It started when I ran to him with the poster, unrolling it to show him, wanting him to see the ship we would escape on. But it was not what I'd expected. His eyes changed instantly when he saw the bright blue letters of "Pleasure Island." They were instantly furious. He looked as if he wanted to rip the poster apart and then stomp on the pieces, as though the color and the words and the ship had no place in Sarajevo and he wanted to drive them out, even from our thoughts. His eyes said there could be no thought of escape. If we had given even a tiny piece of our minds to such thoughts we'd have gone berserk at the first whistling noise, screaming and running into the streets with our fingers in our ears, not caring any longer if one came for us.

Omar said, looking at the poster, "Our time will come." Then he slapped it rudely from my hands and it landed against the base of the wall, flapping and rolling itself up again, as though mocking his futile attempt at aggression.

When Omar heard the laughter of the poster in the silence of our store, he looked like he wanted to cry; and then he did. I've never felt more useless, even with Mira. I didn't know what comfort to offer him. I didn't think I'd done wrong bringing the poster home. I'd wanted to give us hope. I'd wanted to look into his eyes and see that they had gone to the ship and saw everything there as I did: how happy the warm sun, the games we'd play on the gently rolling deck as we watched the cool, inviting waves breaking on the island of our dreams.

That's how I'd imagined it, but his tears took away my dream of us there together. It would not be escape to go alone. Alone is always alone, no matter where it happens. I'd learned that early on from watching Mother.

I was sure if I could just explain to Omar about alone and together—what a difference between them!—about how happy and beautiful our island would be, then he'd help me put the poster on the wall and we could lie under it on the mattress that would no longer smell of the rainy alley where we found it, and there would be a fresh, cool breeze blowing over our bodies as we consoled one another.

But I didn't know how to tell him because his tears disturbed me. It would never do for us to go to the island in tears. It would mean we carried the remains of our lives here with us, and that would be a defeat. It would be like stuffing Mira and the gardens and Adnan and Kemal—

everything—into a suitcase, then carrying it on board the ship, only to have them come back laughing and haunting us when we opened it again. Even if we set it in a corner or tried to hide it away, sooner or later it would be opened, even if by accident, and then they would be all over us before we knew it, accusing us for their going away. We would never be able to rid ourselves of them.

The island must be a clean departure. We'd have to go on board naked, with nothing in our hands, and a smile for each other on our faces.

I wanted desperately for Omar to understand, so I took him by the hand and gave him a gentle tug, inviting him to the mattress with my eyes. He was like a dead weight holding back, even pulling away. Then his tears stopped and he was all over me, nothing but feverish hands furiously groping at me, ripping at my clothes. His breath came to my face in hot waves, and it was rasping and panting, like a wild animal who's hit on its prey. I don't think he knew who I was; maybe he didn't even see me. He could just smell me and wanted me.

I couldn't hold back my anger. I didn't mind that he wanted me; I was glad to be there for him. What I couldn't stand was for his not-seeing eyes to deny my existence, making me nothing. That I was afraid of.

So I slapped him, not maliciously, just so he'd be forced to admit I was there. That brought him up short. A red mark appeared on his face where I'd slapped him, and you could hear the echo of the blow hanging in the quiet air.

SARAJEVO

I'd never done a thing like that before. It was only because I was so afraid of losing myself. My body stiffened a bit, readying itself for his blow in return, and perhaps worse, for the sound of it.

But there was nothing. I looked at his face and still didn't know if his eyes really saw me or not. There'd just been that flash of recognition when I'd slapped him.

Then he said a strange thing that I'll never forget. Quietly, flatly, as though only for himself to hear, he said, "I deserved that." Then he collapsed onto the mattress and hid his face in his hands. My first thought was that he was trying to cover the red mark. I could see why he'd be ashamed that a girl put it there. Or perhaps he was just put off with me. It's the first time I'd refused him.

That's not quite true, however. Now I realize that though my body had always been there in the room, my mind had long ago created the ship, even before I'd seen the poster.

I'd always known it would be blue—before Omar, even before Luka and the Sarajevo. It was one of those beginnings you don't remember. Who knows, perhaps the father I never knew held me on his knee when I was a little girl and told me a story of the ship, and that put the idea in my head. It was even possible he'd been on the ship himself; then when he left he'd gone back to it. In that case, if I could go to the ship now, they'd all be there—Father and Mother and Saša, even Adnan and Mira.

Now I know what I've always wanted is to belong. I'd

wanted to belong to Omar, just as I'd wanted to belong to Luka. I think I'd even wanted to belong with Mother in the tiny little flat that constricted the life out of her.

That's why it had been perfectly normal to set up house with Omar in an abandoned storefront with a door that was off its hinges. It was a form of belonging. We gave ourselves to the store, and it gave us back a sense of home.

Without a place you were nothing. There'd be nothing but space surrounding you, and that would be scary. You'd think being all alone with nothing to contain you would be freedom, but it's just the opposite. That only makes you unconnected, and everything in you is rushing around frantically trying to latch onto something, anything, so you can feel you have a base to grow from. Even Sarajevo, with the hills surrounding it bearing silent witness to the shells raining down on us, is better than nothing. At least there's the certainty of that, that it will continue.

Maybe, too, that's what the soldiers are after when they fire their shells at us. I can imagine the smiles on their faces, like the ones I saw at church, knowing that they belong to something, are a part of something that is greater than themselves, that gives them meaning and takes their aloneness away. How happy they must be!

And our soldiers must feel the same thing to return their fire, so that they can belong to the uniforms they wear and fit comfortably inside them.

If you took their uniforms away and they just stood there looking silly with no purpose and shivering in their nakedness, they'd probably get all scared inside, like I had when I couldn't see myself reflected in the store window because of the blinding light inside. Then they'd have to look for another uniform to put on as soon as possible to take their fear away. And of course they'd have to be different types and colors to separate them into belonging. As soon as you put on one, you create the need for another to exist, so that in the end we all deserve one another.

Looked at that way, everything seems perfectly normal, though I'm sorry for them.

But then I think of the Sarajevo, how I always rushed back there to belong after the going away of Mother, or Mira. And now I see the hotel as a uniform too. Of course you wouldn't recognize it as that at first—the pock-mark shell holes as medals, the windows as buttons, even the door as a belt with its shiny buckle. You'd have to sit outside and really give it some thought, looking at it this way and that, like the abstract paintings Teacher showed us in class, before you could really see it for what it is. But after you saw it, things could never be the same again.

"I deserved that."

At first it seemed I'd thought out loud. But it was Omar, and I almost said, "Of course," as though he'd followed everything I'd been thinking. Then I heard his soft crying, and I sat next to him on the mattress. I wanted to explain to him about uniforms.

I must have done something to startle him, however, because before I could say a thing about the uniforms, he took his hands from his face, and his eyes stared at me, wide and frightened. Then he said another strange thing.

"I was raped."

That froze me, so that I didn't want to tell him anything. I thought he'd read my mind, that somehow he knew about the soldier on Zuc. Perhaps he'd been hiding in the bushes, watching, and he'd only waited to accuse me.

Then I saw how his eyes desperately wanted to go to the blue ship, and I knew he was talking about himself.

For a long time after we made love, we lay side by side in the slowly enveloping dark, our faces pointed upwards toward the ruined ceiling. We lay very close, but without touching, which would actually have been painful. I absorbed the heat of him through his words, and the sound of them was all I could stand.

He'd wanted to be a pilot when he was a young boy. Or an archaeologist—he could never decide which. He had dreams of living in Greece by the sea in a large white house that was open to the sun, and looked like the sun when you tried to stare at its reflected brilliance. He imagined himself standing on a rock that jutted out over the waves, his body and his spirit ready to fly above them, his hair blowing in the wind. He'd only seen the ocean once, but he told me that, unlike the sluggish waters of the Miljacka which must have a beginning and an end, the ocean is wild and free and goes on forever.

He'd wanted to go with it. I felt my nostrils tingling

with salt. I wanted to yell to him that I would go with him, but I was afraid to interrupt.

I was almost glad for his rape that gave him those words—beautiful words; I won't try to repeat them—to tell me of himself. Having known silence that, like the whistling of the shells, makes you want to scream, I luxuriated in the warmth of his words that flooded over me like a blanket of contentment, or the softness of dawn when waking together.

I didn't want to be fourteen anymore, wishing I'd never got my period. I wanted to be a young girl again and to go into the street, or some secret garden, and play games with him. We could dream the same dreams. I would be his navigator, or his assistant. We would board the blue ship hand in hand on a journey first to his beloved Greece, then farther and farther away, to places I'd never even dreamed of. We would sail to Pleasure Island, where the blue of the sea and that of the sky would unite like lovers, and you couldn't tell where one finished and the other began. And like the sea and the sky, we would have no beginning or ending.

I wanted to tell him all those things but couldn't; I was too busy listening. So I took his hot hand and nuzzled my face against the hollow of his neck. I listened not just with my ears, but with all my body. And as he entered through my pores, I felt myself growing to contain him.

Then all at once the sound of his words changed. They were no longer happy sounds filling me, rushing over my eager body like tickling ocean waves whose whitecaps delighted me. They became abruptly harsh and heavy, gaining strength to beat against me, frightening and pursuing.

They were dark words that told me of his family in Tuzla before the war.

They were sad words that told me how his father went to war, stopping in the street before the little house to bravely smile and wave to them as he joined his troop.

They were bitter words that told me of his mother's sudden tears when she opened the letter that informed them of his death.

They were futile words that told me how the soldiers found them in the forest—he with his mother and his sister, who was very beautiful—as they collected firewood.

They were horrible words that told me how the sister screamed and was no longer beautiful when the soldiers laughed as they cut off her hair before they raped her, leaving him to watch while holding him back with their hands and their laughter.

I wanted to drop his hand and stop up my ears, but his words burned and forced me to hear them.

When he told me what they did to his mother before they turned to him, the words lost all meaning and were only anguished, garbled sounds, like Milorad with his mouth full of carrot.

Then he was out of tears, and they were flat, dead words that told me of his own rape. Hearing their sounds, I felt his hurt between my own legs as he said again, "I deserved that." Then I knew that's how I'd been, flat and dead, when the soldier raped me on Zuc. I must have gone away to the blue ship then without even noticing it.

After beating him and calling him a girl, telling him how soft he was, they'd left him to live with his shame, his frozen eyes staring at the darkening sky while the sound of their laughter called after him.

Then there were no words, but I knew why he'd come to the sanctuary of the dead lovers.

"I'm just going out for a walk." They were casual words that told me of his leaving.

I didn't have time to be afraid of being left alone. He was up and gone quickly without looking at me. I felt him going as the weight of him left the mattress, and I wasn't strong enough to hold it down by myself.

Now all I can think of as I lie quietly in the dark, carefully holding myself in, as I have so many other times, is, "He's gone." His favorite color was blue, like the sea.

SANDRA FINISHED COUGHING LAST NIGHT. Yesterday, rather; it wasn't quite dark yet.

We were all there. Nihada took it hardest, though she struggled to remain composed.

I knew all along that her coughing was the beginning of the end of her; we all did, except perhaps Milorad. So I should have been prepared for her silence when it came. She didn't say anything, just opened her eyes a final time, looking up at us without recognizing us. Then she closed them again and coughed weakly, as though apologizing for going away. Then she was silence. Her mouth relaxed a little after that, into a smile.

It was the same blissfully ignorant smile she'd always had, and I felt cold and alone without the rest of her as a shield. I looked from her smile to Luka and for the first time I saw that it had not only been his strength that had held us together, but also the unknowing face of her smile that we could all assume in our secret hearts, without telling the others.

As Luka looked down at her last night, his eyes assumed her silence. Then he walked out without saying anything, and the rest of us were left standing there looking at one another awkwardly out of the corners of our eyes, guilty and not knowing what to do. Nihada took my hand. Her palm was wet.

It was as if we were to blame for being left behind. Luka managed to avoid any contact with that blame by just leaving. As his back went out the door I both envied him and despised him. I would have loved to run from the room myself, but my feet were stuck to the floor, as though encased in concrete. I felt the weight tugging at the rest of me, pulling me down into silence with Sandra. I didn't resist it; I let it take me.

Milorad jerked at my sleeve persistently. Ilija coughed, and after a pause he said, "What will we do with her?" That made us think and stopped the silence. I wanted to run after Luka to find out what we should do, but I didn't think it was right to leave Sandra there alone. Finally, Dejan settled things by turning to Ilija and saying, "You'll stay with her and guard her." Ilija's face got a little scared then, but he did as he was told and sat down first on the edge of the bed, then quickly, as though not to disturb her, on the floor.

We all trooped down the stairs in search of Luka. Our feet made an awful lot of noise, but perhaps they did it on purpose to help us forget the silence of her, which wanted to drag after us, out of the room, then downstairs into the dead lobby and out into the courtyard.

There I looked at the sycamore and was surprised. Even though it was only the beginning of the end of summer, there were dead branches among the living. They

HOTEL

were hard and dry, and rattled in the wind. I thought it strange that they should pick this time to die, like they were already mourning for Sandra.

We found Luka behind the tree, in a corner of the courtyard near the wall. He was digging with a steady, monotonous rhythm, and his eyes still contained the silence of her as he concentrated on the hole he was making in the earth.

We were close behind him, and I could smell the earth. It smelled fresh and moist, but also had the stench of decay. I was frightened and wanted to run back to the room to see if Sandra was still there, but the methodical digging and tossing of Luka's shovel hypnotized me, and I could only watch.

Luka didn't ask for help, and no one offered. In any case, there was only the one shovel. It was almost new. The only other time we'd used it was in the raid on the gardens.

He said nothing till he was finished. All the while we were frozen there, watching the hole grow. As he straightened and turned to us there was sweat on his forehead, but all he said was, "Tomorrow," as though that was all the explanation that was needed.

He dropped the shovel and went inside, leaving us there with the nauseating spectacle of the little ditch waiting to receive her, that was like a mouth gaping in horror.

No one spoke, and finally the others started to drift away, silently, sheepishly. The sight of them shrinking

156

away like that made me furious. I felt the anger rising to my face, and I wanted to yell after them, "It's not her fault!" but I only glared after them. The hole and the pile of fresh dirt next to it just didn't connect. The new earth was loose and moist, but the hole seemed empty and cold and dead. I could see an earthworm wiggling to the top and didn't know if he craved the last warmth of the sun or was just annoyed at having his home disturbed.

I'd thought I was alone. Then I heard a cough, and it startled me. Sandra's was the last cough I'd heard and for a moment I thought she'd come to inspect things for herself. I turned, afraid but wanting to know, and of course it was Milorad who'd remained behind with me.

He looked like a baby, as he always had, but there was knowledge in his eyes. I felt he suddenly understood everything—the war, Sandra's going away—perhaps better than I. I'd always been forced by circumstances to think of myself as grown-up and wise. When Jan had cried at having to go away and leave Radman, it was I who'd consoled her. But now I realized I knew nothing. It was all an act. I felt empty and vulnerable, without a thought in my head, wanting to let everything go out of me until there was nothing left. Then I could start from scratch and construct a new Alma, one who would be stronger and braver and smarter, one who would not feel weak in the knees at the sight of an empty hole in the ground.

But Milorad was there and letting go was impossible. I had no time to think up a new Alma, but had to content

HOTEL

myself with the old one. Needing something in my hands, I took up the shovel and attacked the hole furiously, dirt flying everywhere, and with it my anger and confusion at having him there to see me.

Milorad only said, "Alma?" and that only after I'd been going at it for some time.

I didn't answer until I was out of breath and needed an excuse to stop. My hands were hard against the shovel, trying to make themselves like the wood, as I said without looking at him, "It needs to be larger." Then I felt his soft little hands against mine on the shovel, and mine gladly gave way to his. His body seemed to grow stronger as I watched him digging. And with each shovelful, between my rapid, escaping breath, I saw him becoming a real poet, not just a shadow one.

Perhaps Sandra had been tired and sick for longer than anyone had known. Then it was too late. The only way we could help her now was to make the hole a proper size, that would respect her. Nihada joined us, sitting quietly at the edge of the grave.

I'd never buried anyone before. They'd always just "gone away," or I'd heard of them being buried but hadn't seen it. I didn't like the thought of putting Sandra in the hole, like a dead dog, out of the way. But I could see the reasoning behind it: once she was covered over, she'd be safe and protected there, like a seed that would grow into a flower. I put my hand softly on Nihada's head.

As I listened to the sound of Milorad's shovel struggling against the hard ground, I closed my eyes and thought

158

SARAJEVO

that if he just kept going, there'd be a hole big enough for us all to crawl into. It wouldn't be a grave so much as a cocoon, and when another spring came, we'd burst forth from it with newly formed wings flapping happily against the warm, perfumed air.

Luka came back out once to look at us. I felt his presence and opened my eyes. He looked at us without approval, with nothing at all, really. He might as well have had no eyes, just deep, gaping holes like the one we were digging. He was so still I didn't exactly realize the moment he left. There was just his absence, and grey sky where he'd been.

Milorad finished, turning to Nihada and me, and his expression yelled out, "Come see!" Our closeness gave its approval to him; then we all headed back inside without speaking. He dragged the shovel behind him, like a hobbyhorse that had been ridden to exhaustion. I thought to tell him, "We'll need it tomorrow," but couldn't get it out. I guess he thought of it himself then, because he leaned it carefully against the door before we went in.

With the morning I'm awake early. At first, watching the new rays of light playing at making shadows along my wall, I've forgotten it all, thinking I'm back in the flat with Mother and Saša. There's a butterfly flitting here and there, carefree, jumping happily from one spot on the wall to another. Absorbed in its movement and content in its freedom, I lie quite still on my back with my hands at my sides.

HOTEL

I know all along the butterfly is formed by a ragged bit of curtain moving lightly in the breeze from the open window, but I pretend not to notice, allowing myself to believe it real. It's simply trapped there for a moment to keep me company. Soon, without a doubt, it will escape the flat confines of the wall to soar over me briefly, then out the window to a true freedom.

I watch it for a long time with anxious eyes, waiting for it to break free. I carefully hold my breath in anticipation, only letting it go in whispered little gasps when it becomes absolutely necessary. Oh, how I want it to fly away!

My fascination with the curtain butterfly's struggle is soon interrupted. Luka sticks his head in the door without even knocking, then looks at me in a way that says "It's time." I wait until he closes the door to get up, then follow him out into the silent hall, the false butterfly forgotten.

Everyone comes out of their rooms at once. How strange we all look quietly falling into line, like ghosts going to bury one of their own. It's dangerous, I suppose, staying upstairs in the rooms when most of Sarajevo has taken to its basements like rats. The shells could come at any time to take us away. But we're not animals, Luka says over and over, and we'll not die like them either. He sounds almost sarcastic when he says it, as though he could defeat death by the tone of his voice alone.

I don't have much stomach for what we're about. I'd prefer to start running and keep on until I've found some out-of-the-way place to daydream it all away, but I can't make my feet start to run.

SARAJEVO

We're on the stairs, trooping downwards. Our clothes hang like shrouds around us. I want to pull at mine, ripping them away, until I'm free of them completely, leaving only my naked body, cool and open in the rising light. The line of bodies ahead of me appears to flow down the stairs in little waves, advancing in slow motion. Then I look around straight into Milorad's face which, surprised, doesn't know what to do but smile. That seems grossly out of place. When I look back to the front, I feel terribly dizzy. I'm going to be sick and can't stop it. All their faces become blurred and indistinct, so that I can't make them out. I feel myself floating away from the others, free.

There's a noise like a truck backfiring, very loud, that makes me jump. Then it backfires again, only this time I don't jump because I can see the truck; I'm falling into it. It's tight and cramped and the metal smells cold and damp and dead. Searching, grasping fingers just as cold and dead seem to come out of the walls toward me as the truck jolts to a stop.

That surprises me. The truck should go on forever, taking me away, delivering me, so that I want to scream for it not to stop, for it to keep on going, far, far away.

But it has stopped, hopelessly, in the middle of no-where. There's nothing around me but the cold, mocking silence of the metal, laughing at the stabbing beats of my heart. Then the sliding door in the rear opens, rising with a metallic scraping sound, like a cattle van opening to eject its cargo.

HOTEL

Someone's hand must have opened the door, though I don't see one. But I know I must leave the truck, the cold, dead certainty of it. I can't see out the back, but I go toward it; then there are hands pulling me out. I don't know whether to resist or not. They're pulling at me harder, so I can't resist, no use to resist, and then one slaps me . . .

"Welcome back. You gave us quite a fright."

Milorad's face is almost on top of me, so I can hardly breathe, and I try to push him away. I remember the slap, and I slap at him with both hands, trying to hurt him and punish him. Then I'm yelling at him, "Don't get in the truck!"

That only brings their laughter, however, and Milorad says, "There is no truck, Alma. You're only imagining things."

The hardness of the floor beneath me intrudes to tell me I'm flat on my back on the landing. Everyone is gathered around me. I see white floating over me and I don't know what it is. It's only after Milorad's embarrassed cough and the downcast, apologetic look on his face that I know it's Sandra wrapped in a sheet, making her look larger than she was in life. They're carrying her outside, away from the safety of the Sarajevo to the alone of the hole in the courtyard, where perhaps she'll be afraid all by herself.

We were never actually friends, Sandra and I. I always saw her as a rival until the last, when she developed the cough and Luka immediately gave her up, resigning her even then to the hole. But I don't want her to go. It leaves me cold and frightened. Maybe it's because all the others went away to be buried. We're left to dispose of Sandra ourselves. And that's what it is, a disposal, not a burial at all. That's why I wanted to make the hole larger, to give her more significance. When she got the cough she should have just wandered away like Mother and Saša, or found herself a hospital, like Adnan, who'd managed to get his legs blown off to relieve us of his burden. But she failed to think ahead. Now we're left with the dead fact of her to cover over. Even after it's finished we'll know she's out there in the courtyard, a silent witness beneath the silent dirt.

They've gone down the stairs and outside, carrying the rigid coldness of her. Even Milorad finally dropped my hand and ran after them. That gives me the creeps. I don't want to be left here alone. That would be like trading places with her. I've never been so alone as here on the stairs, in the dead silence of the Sarajevo.

I want the sun and, grasping at the thought of the butterfly on my wall, I know it must be there, outside, if only I can run fast enough through the lobby and out the double doors to catch it. That's all I think of as I sprint across the carpeted floor and fling open the doors with a bang. For a moment as brief as a single whispered word, I imaging I'll open them to find Mother, and she'll be surrounded by flowers and, smiling, hold out her arms to me, which I'll not even think to refuse. After we've spent the

HOTEL

day together, at the Café-Bar Lisac with cola and ice cream, eating and laughing our fill, we'll walk home smiling, hand in hand.

Mother's not there beside the hole with the others. But Milorad and Nihada are, wanting me at their side, where they're waiting with Sandra stretched out on the ground next to her hole.

There're no flowers. I'm only conscious of the dead branches in the sycamore as I cross the courtyard. Everything is very quiet, as first Luka and then the others look up, listening. I must be quite a sight, so I think it's me they're looking at so strangely, but then I hear it too—the long, low whistling sound that keeps coming. It seems to be searching for us, but I can't turn and look for it. Acknowledging it would just make us easier targets.

It gets louder still, crying out, and can't be ignored. I want to stop up my ears but my hands are useless. There's something in Luka's eyes that's not fear or anticipation, something I've never seen before.

I turn to try to see what he sees, just in time to see part of the Sarajevo's roof explode, like a tiny volcano spewing out its guts. We've been hit many times before, only it's always been against the front of the building. This is different, like being personally violated. Before I have time to really take it in there's another hit, only now I have the impression of the roof throwing up, like the first one made it sick.

"Hurry!" It's Luka. The others all want to run, but his voice holds them there, demanding they put her in the hole and cover her over before they allow themselves to be afraid.

They drop her hurriedly in the hole. I hear her land, *plop!* in the bottom. Then Milorad grabs the shovel.

"No! Wait!" I'm surprised and delighted to find myself obeyed. I run back toward the hotel, accompanied by another low, ominous whistle. But I don't think about it because I'm running too fast through the lobby (the whistling), up the stairs (the whistling), into the safety of my room (it's stopped), where my hand reaches purposefully underneath my mattress to find the scarf Luka offhandedly gave me long ago. Then I'm back down the stairs with a jump (there's a heavy, shaking thud on the roof), and I'm crossing the lobby with plaster falling about me. Then I'm free of the hotel, just as the sun comes happily from behind a cloud. I echo its happiness to find them still standing there, waiting. Other than Milorad, and Omar, it's the first time anyone's ever paid any attention to what I've said.

No one says anything as I drop the scarf on top of Sandra's sheet, and watch it float downward, like a dying butterfly. Then Luka's dead face gives a nod to release them from their stillness. They go at it with the shovel and their hands, digging like moles, furiously anxious to get her out of sight. Only Milorad and Luka stand aloof; Luka because he's the chief, and Milorad, I guess, because he thinks he's done his part to drag the shovel to the hole. I put my hands comfortingly on Nihada's shoulders.

It's only a few sad seconds before the scarf is completely

covered and out of sight. It's like I never ran to get it, like it never even existed.

Without looking at the others I go to the sycamore and sit beneath it with my back pressed hard against the trunk. I'm glad my name is no longer one of those carved into it. If anyone finds it after the war, I don't want them to know I was here for this.

I'm shaking as the sun goes behind the clouds again, like I've been cold forever. Even Nihada sitting beside me can't stop my shivering. The others are huddled together in a line against the courtyard wall.

The summer is dying, with Sandra.

Even though the shelling doesn't start again, our roof is ruined, leaving us naked. We make the silent move to the basement. No one, not even Luka, gives the word. It's just a general, unspoken consensus. I help, but it's automatic, without thinking, like a robot with batteries.

Luka said we'd never be like the rats; and now we are.

PART
THREE

J AN'S BACK!
I haven't seen her yet myself, but it's true. This morning I was carrying a plastic jug of water through the lobby and down to the basement when Ilija passed me without speaking, then called out to me, "Your friend's back." My heart jumped when he said it; I almost dropped my jug. First I thought he meant Omar, but he knows nothing of Omar. So I knew that it must be Jan. When I turned to him, he confirmed it: "The reporter, the one who writes about us." Then the jug seemed less heavy, and a joy to carry.

We don't have our own rooms in the basement, like we did upstairs. When we first moved down here everyone just picked a spot and settled in. That made me uncomfortable and fidgety. One morning I was busy in my corner and Milorad, curious about what I was doing, came to inspect a rope I'd strung between the two walls.

It wasn't something I'd thought out. The sight and feel of all of us together like that depressed me, and I wanted to do something about it. We looked at each other silently, then I took a blanket and draped it over the rope, shutting him out. First he was there; then he was gone and I was

169

alone, like an eclipse. I heard his laugh from the other side. There were movements in the blanket where his hands poked at it. The blanket was alive and laughing, like a puppet show. Then his laughing face moved the blanket aside to play a game with me. Only I didn't feel like playing. Gruffly, I pushed his face away behind the blanket and out of my space, denying him.

I heard his laughter again and that made me mad. When he stuck his head through again, I slapped him. The surprise on his face! He didn't pull back right away, so I raised my hand again and that made him retreat quickly. I wasn't trying to be mean; I just didn't want him there. But he must have thought it still a game, because he continued to poke at my blanket and then started pulling it slowly off the rope, deliberately trying to provoke me. So I waited till his shape lingered for a second in the blanket, then kicked at it savagely, with all the force of my indignation. He let out a howl and began hopping around like a crippled insect, holding his thigh and complaining, "She's trying to kill me!" He only stopped when everyone began to laugh. Then he came back, rubbing his thigh, but now he only wanted to inspect my blanket and ask me why.

He caught me up short, and I didn't have an answer for him. All I could do was stammer and then burst out with, "Because . . . I'm big now."

Everyone laughed again, but this time at me, and I wished I had never even thought of it.

Luka roused himself, coming forward and looking at

SARAJEVO

the blanket, then touching it with his fingertips. It was the first time he'd shown any interest in things since Sandra's funeral. There was even a little of the old fire in his eyes when he said, "It's a good idea." That impressed Ilija and the others, who were happy to see him that way. They all went scurrying about to find some rope, and in a moment there was another blanket hanging across the opposite corner where our lone portable toilet was. Ilija held it proudly aside for Luka, but he'd already lost interest, forgetting the whole thing. He went to sit alone in the center of the room, looking at his fingers, the length of the nails, but staring past them at the empty floor.

Ilija pretended not to notice, and went behind the blanket smiling. Soon we heard him let loose with his water, followed by giggling. Then he came out, embarrassed, and said, "It's hard when there's someone waiting." Then all the others wanted to go. Only when it was my turn, I became obstinate and taciturn as I'd tired of their game. I went behind my own blanket, that had started it all, and refused to come out, even when they began chanting, "Alma! Alma!" I can be very stubborn, like a mule, when I get something in my head.

It was only much later, in the afternoon, when they'd all quieted down, that I pulled my blanket aside, walked calmly across the room through them, and entered the bathroom without hesitation. It's very quiet and pleasant to do your business in peace, even if you can't flush each time. The smell makes you want to hurry. If the war is ever finished and I have my own place, the first day I'm

171

there I'm just going to sit and flush as often as I want until there's no smell even in my memory.

When I came outside the blanket again, everyone except Luka was standing there waiting, and they all let out a cheer. I didn't pay them any attention, however, going back to my space to be by myself. Afterwards, to pick at me, they started calling it, "Alma's toilet," but I didn't let it get to me. I'm too big for that and, anyway, I'm a little proud, because it was my idea.

That's the first day I started drawing the pictures. I don't know where I got the idea. There have always been scraps of paper about and, sitting behind my blanket, I found a piece of charcoal on the floor in the corner and just started doodling while they were calling for me to come out. Partly it was an attempt to spite them, but also because I just didn't have anything else to do. I liked the comforting feel of the charcoal in my fingers, and only later did I notice my picture was taking shape. I looked at it this way and that, trying to make it out. At first I thought it could be maybe a bowl of fruit, but then I drew more and I recognized it as the sycamore in the courtyard. Its leaves were dying, just like now with the coming of winter.

The first snow was just the other day. It wasn't much, just a few flakes in the courtyard. After I'd finished watching it, I went back to the privacy of my corner and added the snow to my picture of the sycamore. It made the whole thing seem colder, however, so that it made me shiver before I put it away.

SARAJEVO

I'm getting quite good. Not anything like professional, but it pleases me to look at them. There's one of the front of the Sarajevo. It looks very distinguished with its shell marks. It's a good thing you can't see from the picture the state the roof is in now. That would be embarrassing. It was a pleasure to draw the picture of our hotel. I even hummed a little while I worked at it, pleased to watch the progress my hand was making all by itself. Mother would be surprised, I think, to discover that I have a talent.

I did one of Kemal's house too. It would have been impossible before, when I only had the charcoal. But one day I remembered I'd seen a box of colored chalks left behind by one of the hotel's guests before the war. I'd come across it while rummaging in a large drawer behind the desk in the lobby, but then I had no use for it. I didn't have any hope it would still be there when I went back to look for it, but there it was, undisturbed. Then I had marvelous colors to do Kemal's house justice, making it live again, as it once did when he was in it.

I have a bright blue piece of chalk and with it I drew a picture of Omar's ship, wondering if he's on it, hoping that he is. It would be nice to go back to our room to see if the poster's still there, but the shelling's been getting worse and mostly we're afraid to go out, though no one says so.

I'm not afraid anyone will discover my pictures. They're tucked up in the folds of my other blanket, and anyway, after the incident of slapping Milorad, no one has given a thought to poking their head behind my grey blanket wall. I could create my own fairy castle there and no one would ever be the wiser!

One day I looked at my pictures and was surprised to find that they are all of places or things. There are no people among them, not one face. I didn't plan it that way; I just never thought to do one. I'm not sure I can. When I look at people it's not their faces I concentrate on, or even see, but only their bodies moving like headless puppets. Sometimes I have to shake my head to stop myself from imagining them as merely pairs of arms and legs, flapping grotesquely in order to make themselves seem real. Bosnians are noted for their humor and ability to laugh, but I don't feel it now. It's been replaced by a dull numbness that I'm aware of, but can't shake.

I have a secret. It's a surprise for Jan. As soon as I found out that she was back, right after I deposited my water jug in a corner of the basement, I went behind my blanket and started to draw, only this time it was a face. It was just something I felt like doing for her. I don't know how it will turn out, or if she'll even like it. If it ends up badly I can always tear it up.

It will be my face, but I've only just started. I want to give Jan something. She's been gone so long, longer than just the summer, it seems. Maybe she's just here to say hello and will be gone again before I'll even have a chance to tell her about Mira, or my birthday. I can't just blurt it out, the first time I see her. I want to feel she's interested and give her a chance to ask me questions. Then I can show her how much I've grown by the way I answer. I'll be calm and matter-of-fact about everything. I'll not slip up and sing out for ice cream and cola either, as if they were available.

If she asks about Mother, I'll just shrug and say she's "gone away" with the others. I'll simply tell her that Radman's scarf is with Mira. I know she'll understand the necessity of it. I'd like to tell her I gave Luka's scarf to Sandra to hold onto, but then Jan might want to come to the courtyard to see where she's buried, and that's off-limits for grownups. That's Luka's rule anyway, and it still has the force of law, even though he doesn't show much interest in anything lately.

Perhaps he's sick; his eyes look funny. Since we moved to the basement he seems to have given up. He sends Ilija and Dejan out for errands, and it's only occasionally that he'll go out onto the terrace overlooking the courtyard.

I found him there the other day. I went there to toss out the shallow pan of dirty water we all wash in. Just as I came outside, the sun broke through the clouds and the grey went away. The sun was directly behind him, and when he turned toward me I couldn't see his face at all. There was just a body sitting there, immobile, as though it knew the sun would come at that instant to provide it with a face and a golden smile.

I blinked several times; then when my eyes adjusted, the sun had moved and taken him away, out past the sycamore, staring at the bare earth tramped down over Sandra. You can still see footmarks in the dirt. Neither of us said anything. I could hear a few birds calling and wished to be with them. For the first time I noticed how bare Sandra's grave was without a marker.

Luka was quiet for so long that I began to get uncomfortable. I wanted to say something to keep my mouth from getting dry. Then, just as I opened my mouth, not really knowing what was coming out, I heard Luka's voice say, quietly but distinctly, "Useless"—just the one word, that's all. I was glad he'd said it. It relieved my mouth of the need to say something, taking me off the hook. He turned and headed back across the courtyard, and as I followed I wondered if the same thing would have come out of my mouth if I had spoken instead. When he got to the terrace he hesitated as though the sun was in his face, but it wasn't, so I took his arm gently and led him up the steps and inside. His arm shivered a little when I touched him; then it relaxed.

Of course I'm going to see Jan. I could probably just wait for her to find me, but she'll be busy writing her stories and it might take a long time. Ilija says she's not where she was before. That building's been destroyed. He saw her come out of a newer one not far from where the train station used to be.

I know I can find her. I'm going in the morning, when it's still a little dark. I don't know what to wear. My hair is longer than when she saw me last, since Mother isn't here to cut it. But it doesn't look too bad, except it's more tangled than usual. Jan will be certain to see that, but then she'll smile and want to brush it for me like before, and of course I'll let her.

I'm not afraid to go to her. It's no more dangerous than anything else. It's all a matter of where you happen to be. You could be in one place and safe, or another and the shells would come for you and take you away. There's no way to know. I've overheard some say, "It's God's will," then watched them make the sign of the cross; but I just don't see it. The others had just as much right to be in a safe place as I, perhaps more when you think about the beauty of Kemal's sightless eyes. If we were all born with eyes like that, then there'd be no need to hide in cellars from one another. How different that would be! We could all be outside with the sunlight warm on our faces, and I wouldn't have to worry about being plain anymore because there'd be no one to take notice. Then I might be a princess because of my words, or simply because I was someone's friend, or perhaps even because of my pictures when I'm good enough.

That's too much to think about. As I sit in my corner behind my blanket with my charcoal, it's enough to concentrate on the lines and shading, hoping I get a little of it right. Sometimes I still feel as though I'm just doodling. I want Jan to be able to recognize me from my picture, to note how I've grown, that I'm no longer "little Alma." At the same time I don't want to look too serious. I don't want her to get the idea that I'm asking for sympathy. I've nothing to be sorry about, except perhaps for living in a cellar instead of in the light with a room all to myself. But I have my blanket wall now, and I'm thankful for that. It's not to hide behind, but only to have a little privacy.

I've got the general outline I think. Does my nose really look like that? I don't know what to do about the eyes. I've purposely left them to the last. The hair was easy, nothing to it really. It has nothing to say, just lying there straight and flat. But eyes are different because they tell so much. Eyes can be laughing or sad, smiling or vacant or horrible, or just nothing at all, like Luka's have become.

I'm not getting any closer to the way the eyes should look. Then I get an idea and, pushing aside the blanket, I walk resolutely to the middle of the basement and pick up an empty plastic jug. Casually I start up the stairs. Milorad's busy playing marbles with Dejan; he looks up at me for a moment with curiosity, then goes back to his game. I'm relieved at not having to answer any questions, so I almost skip up the stairs.

I'd forgotten how quiet it is now in the lobby. Before, we used to run back and forth at all angles, but since we've taken to the cellar there's just the immense stillness of desertion. There's a bathroom in a corner, and I slip inside as quickly and silently as possible, not wanting to be detected.

It smells musty. It's strong enough to make me want to pinch my nose, but in a few seconds I'm used to it. The shiny white tiles glare at me. They're like pairs of eyes with big square-rimmed glasses, really peering at me. But I don't let it bother me as I go straight to the big mirror over the sinks. I take a deep breath and, leaning on the cold ceramic sink with both hands, look into the mirror.

There I am, looking back at myself. It's not what I thought, though. I'm just as uncertain as ever. What sort of eyes are those? Not smiling or laughing, that's for sure, but not necessarily sad or defeated either. They are not Kemal's eyes, or Clarisse's, that I'd have been happy with, but they have a calmness that I like. It makes me feel good to look into them, especially since the ones in the mirror seem accepting of mine, like a twin sister's might be.

I spend a long time looking at the eyes in the mirror, so that when finally I hear a sound from somewhere outside and make a move, I'm uncertain at first which is the real me.

No one's about when I open the bathroom door and head back downstairs. I seem so matter-of-fact as I re-place the still empty jug with the others, that no one even thinks to question me. Milorad doesn't even look up.

In the corner behind the blanket I have no trouble drawing in the eyes, getting it right the first time without the slightest miscue. The only thought I have when I've finished and carefully rolled it up is, "Jan will be pleased."

It's snowing, the first real snow of the winter. It's not re-ally winter until it snows, I don't care what anyone says. It's not inevitable until the snow comes to say, "There's no going back." When it covers everything there's nothing to do but wait for spring.

It's coming down hard, which makes it more difficult to

HOTEL

be seen. After closing the front door of the hotel behind me, I can barely see the street. It's only the sounds of the people hidden there that are intelligible to me. I hear them becoming through the snow, which is like a lace veil surrounding and protecting me. Then, quickly, there are faces and hands and arms and legs moving rapidly to keep warm, or just in play. I'd like to make a picture of it, and must remind myself later, when I have the chance. I can see in my mind how it would be. The snow, of course, would dominate, with patches of sky here and there. Then there'd be pieces of people popping in and out of the white, just like I see them now. Some would be smiles; others taciturn and moody; still others quick flashes of movement on their way somewhere. There'd just be a splash of color where a person moved through the picture. Of course there'd be the hills above the snow, just lying there and waiting, like in real life.

I wonder if all cities have rows of hills around them, like jaws waiting to swallow them up. Mostar is the only other city I've seen, and that was so long ago I hardly remember, but I think it had its hills too. I've been to a few small towns around Sarajevo that were flat, but they don't really count. I think it has to be a real city to have hills. Without the hills there'd be no place to mount the guns. But without the city there'd be no one to shoot at, or at least not enough to make it worthwhile anyway. You can see that the city and the hills need each other.

As I go down the steps there's a *whoosh!* coming out of the snow that becomes two young boys sledding on a large piece of cardboard. The one in back has his arms around the other, who's yelling at the top of his voice. There's no stopping them; if I'd been in the way they'd have run me down. What a luxury they're taking for themselves! The cardboard should have been used for fuel. Almost certainly someone will be cold because of their extravagance. I want to cry out to them to stop and come to their senses, but I don't. The cry stops inside me and then just dies as Milorad rushes out the door and past me clutching his own sheet of cardboard, almost knocking me down in his haste to join the others. He laughs at that. I start to get angry, but he has such a silly look on his face that I involuntarily return his laugh instead. Let loose in the air, it's like a balloon floating away, carrying the happy sound with it. If I laughed hard enough, maybe it would make a balloon that could float all the way over the hills . . .

Milorad stumbles on the bottom step, letting out a curse. Maybe it's from the limp, or maybe because of the floppy blue sneakers he still insists on wearing even though we've found others more his size. He says they're good luck, but I really believe he thinks he'll grow faster to fit them and then he'll be a man. The limp is all in his head, too. The cut healed nicely and there's no reason for him to go limping about now except that he's used to it. Maybe he got some comfort from the attention it brought him and he doesn't want to lose it now.

I pass him on the steps and my hand gets the urge to tousle his unruly hair, just to feel the softness of it. But feeling himself too big for that, he pulls away with an anguished, "Alma!" So I continue silently on, reluctantly, until his excited cry comes to me, "Come play!" Then I look back to see him beaming, the cardboard in his hands, like a new toy he'd got for Christmas. I can't help smiling when I see the loose jumbled mess that he calls a knot, securing the oversized sneakers. He's never learned to tie them properly. I used to do it for him. He'd come to me silently and just sit there, waiting. Perhaps he secretly wishes that I'll do it again now. Instead, I only call back to him, "Later!" before I disappear in the snow. I know their cardboard sleds will have made a runway that's fast enough to take your breath away by the time I get back from seeing Jan. And of course Milorad's sneakers will still need tying.

It's good to be lost in the snow. I could be on my way to anywhere. If I try to think of nothing else, all I'm aware of is being surrounded by the snow. I'm not in the street at all. There are no buildings lying in ruins, embarrassed by their scars. I'm on a forest path, and out beyond the snow I can hear birds calling for me to follow. They're my friends, that's why they're calling for me. I've always been good with animals, even though I've never had one of my own. Once, when I was little, I brought home a cat, a stray, but Mother wouldn't let me keep it in the flat, so I left scraps for it in the alley under our window and would see it every day until one day it didn't come. Even so, I still left a little something for a week, until I was sure it

SARAJEVO

wouldn't come again. I've always had an attraction for things that need taking care of. Milorad, for instance.

The birds are calling louder now, shrilly, like there's something wrong. There must be something out there in the snow disturbing them. But when I peer into the snow all I get for my trouble is the cold wet of the flakes when they sting my face. If enough of them hit you in the face it's like anesthesia almost. And that's a good feel, because it takes you away. I wish Sandra'd had anesthesia when she began to finish her coughing. But at least she had the same smile she'd always had. Perhaps that was like anesthesia too. Maybe it's Sandra the birds are calling for now. Perhaps she's even gone away to become one of them. I wonder if you become a bird when you go away, and sing for the others who are left behind. It comforts me to think of Mother as a bird flying overhead, calling for me.

The sound of the birds is no longer in front of me, but behind. I turn to look for them through the snow, and then their calling becomes one long, shrill, tormented whistle and I think, "How stupid." I should have known all along that the birds were afraid of the shells and that's why they were calling.

The whistling finishes itself with a *pow!* somewhere off in the direction of the Sarajevo. At the same time I think I see Milorad through the snow. A truck that looks familiar has stopped directly in front of the hotel, and he's scrambling almost joyfully into the back of it. He turns to look at me, and I can see his face clearly. Then I get cold and scared because I recognize the truck. It's the same one that trapped me in my dream! My voice rings out loud across the emptiness and silence of the snow: "Don't get in the truck!"

Right away I feel like a fool. Some people on the opposite street corner are staring at me. Then they start to come toward me. It's them I've yelled at; there was no truck. They must think me an idiot, and I don't want to explain, so I run off fast down the street, toward Jan.

It's almost stopped snowing. There's the orange booth of the train station. Before, I always thought the orange was showy and out of place, even silly. Now I'm glad for it; it generates warmth, even though its trains no longer have anywhere to go.

Once, when Jan was here before, I came with her to take pictures. There was a big crowd, all pushing to get on the train; some were even cursing and crying. Finally the train was full, really packed. They were helpless inside its tin shell with no room to move. Then there was a long wait. Jan moved about snapping pictures from all angles, with me tagging after her. Each time I heard the camera click I closed my eyes briefly and tried to fix the picture there. One snap was of a train window. On the inside was a mother's face and those of her two children. Her face was flat and expressionless; those of the children were wide-eyed and quizzical. On the outside of the window was a father's head and shoulders. It was just the back of his head. I couldn't see his face, but I could imagine it because his arms and hands were outstretched, with the fingers pressing against the glass before trailing down hopelessly to his sides.

Another snap was of an old grandmother stoically holding a child against her while being turned away. There were so many snaps I don't remember them all. The loudspeaker announced several times that the train was going to depart. Once the engine even started up. Then it stopped again and after another long wait some men in uniform boarded the train and went the length of it. Then everyone began to get off. Some were crying. I even heard a few screams, but most were only silent. I saw the father again. Now he was with the mother and children. He had a child's hand in one of his and his arm around the mother. He seemed happier now, but also sad. The mother was just as stone-faced as ever.

Jan explained that something had prevented the train from going away. They would try again another day. However, she was still glad for the pictures. I had my pictures too, in my head. Looking back at them later, carefully studying the faces, I decided they knew even then there wouldn't be any departure. Their faces, though more composed, reminded me of the anguish of Omar's look when he'd cried out, "There's no escape!" Their silence said the same thing.

Now the train just sits there, alone. For a short time it was used as an aid station, but that was abandoned. It was too open. The snow on top looks like a weight, holding it down.

HOTEL

Jan's building is somewhere along the street. But how can I expect to find her? I can't simply ask in all the offices of all the buildings. That could take forever.

I'm stuck there to the street, stupid and defeated, watching the last flakes of snow fall, when suddenly the taped glass doors of the building across the street open and there's Jan! The sight of her makes my eyes shine and my heart race. Right away I've forgotten Mira, and the carrots, and Omar, even my birthday. I'm no longer fourteen but still thirteen. I haven't seen Sandra finish coughing, or helped dig her grave. I could even still have a doll if I wanted one. It's as if Jan never went away on a plane, never left Sarajevo at all. She only came here to this building, and now I've found her.

I run across the street. My picture is inside my coat pocket, protected from the snow. My cold hand reaches inside to touch the warmth of it there, and I'm happy to have drawn it for her and to be carrying it to her at last.

The door opens again and Radman is there beside Jan, and that makes me happy too. I'm only a little sad that I didn't find her first and have her to myself for a while, to tell her about Omar and her scarf and all the other things. But I'm just glad she's come back.

Radman catches her arm and turns her toward him, and their faces aren't happy like they should be. Jan's face is angry and loud; Radman's, tired and sad. I don't think they're going to kiss. Then Jan slaps him and he drops her arm. I not only hear the slap, I feel it too, hot and heavy on my cheek. I remember Mother slapping me once in a way that said, "Go away!" That must be what Jan's slap says too, because Radman looks at her blankly. Then he leaves her, slowly walking down the street. I expect Jan to call after him to come back, and I listen for it, but she doesn't. I don't understand, but I know it's over between them. I feel I'm to blame for giving her scarf to Mira so that I don't have it to return to her now. Perhaps he asked about it and didn't understand why she'd given it to me to keep for her return. I'd like to run after him to explain, but he's gone, so I run up to Jan instead, pulling out my picture happily as I go to her.

Before I reach her some other reporters burst out of the building, surrounding her. They all have papers and cameras like Jan, and some of them are getting into a car as she waits her turn. I'll have to hurry!

I push my way through to her. Pulling at the sleeve of her coat, I know that in a minute she'll take me in her arms and hug me as before. She turns and looks, first straight over my head, then down into my face. I push my picture at her already-full hands, and Jan! has almost formed on my happy lips. Her eyes are on the picture and I know she's going to break into a smile and hug me, but before she can, another voice, that's hard and hurried, calls out from the car, "Jan!" Then Jan quickly follows the voice into the car, and when she does so my picture flutters uselessly down to the pavement as the car pulls away.

I see only the back of her head in the car. After it's gone I look for my picture. It's lying silently on the pavement,

HOTEL

face up, but there's a muddy footprint over the face that makes me feel dirty.

I'd like to push someone out of my way, but they've all gone off in their cars. All that's left is a wrinkled old bag lady loitering near the door, looking for warmth or a hand-out, and I can't push her because she's so like myself.

I sadly pick up my once proud picture, with the bag lady watching me curiously. I put it in my pocket as casually as I can, then cross the street the way I came.

When I pass the orange of the station booth again, all I can think of is how ugly it is.

On the way home to the Sarajevo I console myself with the thought that perhaps the picture wasn't a good like-ness and that's what threw her off. Or maybe it was my hair. It could have been my hair.

I pass an alley and hear noises and then a *meow!* There I find a big calico cat rummaging hungrily in a turned-over can. For one happy moment I think it's the cat from my childhood that's come back, so I pick it up. But when it scratches me I know it couldn't be the same, or if so, it failed to recognize me too, so I drop it and walk away. I can't see my face, but it feels as stiff and beaten as the faces of the people on the train when they realized it wasn't going to move and there was nothing to do but si-lently crawl away homeward, like snails.

I brighten a little when I think about Milorad on the steps trying to tie his sneaker. He'll have made a mess of it and will need me to help him. There's that to look forward to anyway.

I DON'T KNOW HOW TO DRAW the mute's sound, what color to use, or what shape to give it. But it will have to be grey, or brown, or black. Of that I'm sure.

As for the shape, perhaps it's just as well to draw a circle and fill it in with letters approximating the sound, like in a cartoon. The letters will have to be *ugh!* or something similar that sounds flat, ugly, brutal, and senseless. But still, there'd be no real sound unless someone came along to read it and give it their voice. It would look funny to have the letters there all alone with no one screaming them. Yes, that's right, screaming. Over and over, hoarsely, until there's nothing left and sound is gone, used up.

I'd do it if I could. But I know to let myself go like that would mean a breakdown of everything, all the fragile pieces of myself that I've carefully held together to avoid just such a collapse. Now I'm thankful to have learned that from watching Mother in her silent waiting.

It's better this way. Probably we all do it. We all must have our little collections of odds and ends, like Mira did, to establish who we are and to help preserve our sanity.

It's fine for me to draw. That's one of my pieces. But to

189

HOTEL

go running about in the street screaming "ugh!" would be a sure sign of insanity. At least it would be taken that way. Then I'd be branded, like Mira, and it would be hard to shake.

It's alright for the mute, since it's the only sound he can make. In any case, he wasn't screaming. Probably he'd seen it before somewhere. It must have happened many times that I don't know about. That makes it seem not so bad, normal almost.

Normal is sane. The more a thing is repeated, the more normal it is, like the shelling, which has become an every-day part of us.

It was abnormal for Milorad and his friends to be play-ing in the snow like children. They should have known better. It's just not done anymore, so the normal is re-moved from it.

So, in a way, no one should be surprised that normal came to take them away in the form of the shell. It was to be expected. What's funny, if you think of it, is that only forty-six shells fell on the city that day, making it seem odd, or less likely in any event, that one of them should have come for Milorad.

Once they made the childish decision to laugh and yell and sled on their pieces of cardboard, thinking the snow would protect them, it was inevitable what would hap-pen. One could almost have predicted it. Why I didn't think about it when I passed Milorad on the steps, I don't know. I should have scolded him right then, forcing him back inside. Then there'd have been no target in the street to attract the killing shells.

At first, when I returned from seeing Jan and found the mute pointing out the red patches of snow, giving them all the explanation they needed with his *ugh!*, I didn't connect things up, though I suppose it should have been obvious.

The first thought I had was that someone had lucked upon some stray animals—pigs came to mind—and had butchered them right there in front of the Sarajevo. How convenient! Now we'd all have meat to eat.

It was only after I saw the sneaker that I began to understand. It was all by itself, like someone had tossed it aside without thinking. Then I thought, "Milorad's lost his sneaker again," and I smiled at his misadventure. If only he'd tied it properly! I could have retrieved it and taken it inside to him, but that would only have set him fuming that he'd forgotten it. Better to let him discover it for himself.

The mute started out with his *ugh!* again, only this time I got the impression it was directed at me alone. His eyes were on me as he pointed again to the red snow. It looked like crushed ice with cherry flavoring added, and should have made me thirsty for a soda, but it didn't. Instead, my lips stuck together.

Dejan and Ilija and Nenad are gone with Milorad. Daniel, Milorad's school friend, was the only one not taken

HOTEL

away. He had a cut on his forehead and an ugly wound on his arm when we went to see him in the hospital. He'd never been allowed to become an Jevo because of reasons known only to Luka. Daniel's only eleven and smaller than Milorad, but he's very brave and never complains. Perhaps Luka saw him as a rival if the war should go on forever.

They'd been all together in a clump, laughing with one voice. They probably never knew a thing. Milorad had turned to the others, yelling, "One more go!" Then the shell came with a blinding flash to do its damage, and the laughter was sucked out of them forever.

In the hospital Daniel said, blank-faced, "Milorad's head was blown completely off." Then he looked away before he went on, "I didn't think to look to see if I could find it."

There'd been no screaming. Actually, everything was quiet. Daniel lay there, not moving, until he felt hands on him. They put him in an ambulance and the others in back of a truck. Daniel said he'd started to complain, to tell them that they must all go together. But then he'd realized that they were different from him now, so he didn't say anything.

When he told us that, calmly, as though it were ordinary, I thought of my vision of Milorad climbing in back of the truck, and blamed myself for not being able to warn him. I wanted to cry, but there was nothing there. My eyes were like deserts whose fragile springs had dried up long ago, without my even knowing it.

192

SARAJEVO

The last thing Daniel said to us when it was time for us to leave him was, "What did we do to them? Why do they hate us?" He said it plaintively, his eyes begging for an answer. But there was none, at least none I could think of, so we marched silently past his eyes and out the door.

Just before we went out, Daniel called to us from his bed, "I want to be an Jevo, like Milorad!" That made my mouth and throat go dry, like I'd just swallowed a handful of sand.

We never saw Milorad again. The next day Ilija and Dejan and Nenad were laid out in a room at an abandoned school. They let what's left of the Jevos in to see them because we were friends. Ilija's little sister, Nihada, didn't come. No one asked her. After the shell exploded she ran out to see what had happened. When I returned to find the mute pointing out the bloody snow, I searched until I found Nihada sitting alone in the courtyard under the sycamore. Even though there was a break in the snow she was shivering. I took her back inside and warmed her with a blanket. Then I went back to the store Omar and I had shared. My dancer was still there in her drawer in the cabinet. I took her to Nihada and demonstrated how she danced. There was a flicker of gratitude in Nihada's eyes as she took the dancer from me. I kissed Nihada on her hair.

Luka didn't come, either, to bid his friends farewell, but remained in the silent tomb of the hotel. I wondered if his eyes were open or closed.

HOTEL

He hadn't even come outside the day before when the mute kept on with his "ugh!" like he already knew about the bloody snow and the contorted shapes that went with it. He just sat inside, Buddha-like on the stairs, waiting for it to happen, expecting it.

He was sitting on the stairs when I ran inside to tell him. Out of breath, I'd started to blurt it out, "Milorad has gone away!" but I'd stopped when I saw Luka's face: he already knew. He looked like a ghost, a quiet, used-up ghost. That made me sad for him, even as I hated him.

Standing before his acceptance, I was like the mute, who was denied the benefit of words, the naming of things. That's a horrible feeling. When you can attach a name to something, even something horrible, it makes it concrete, and that makes it bearable. It's easier to say, "Milorad is dead," than "Mother has gone away." There's no name for just vanishing, so it has no validity. Even though they'd taken away the bodies of Milorad and the others when I'd returned, at least the bloody snow was there to tell of their going.

Luka said, "We're alone." The sound of it frightened me. It was flat, unexpected, with a complete lack of emotion, like dead leaves falling and hitting against one another. Then when the sound had gone, a feeling of total isolation crept into me.

Frantically I looked around the lobby. I desperately needed for someone else to be there, but there was no one. It was then I knew he didn't just mean we were alone in the hotel: no one was coming to help us, ever.

SARAJEVO

I wanted to run again. But, really, there was no place to run to. And besides, it was what he wanted. Denied the relief of running for himself because of his position as chief, he could only sit and wait, hoping someone else would do it for him.

He'd become like one of those molded, chocolate figures with nothing inside. If you broke one open, it no longer had any definable shape to it. You couldn't even guess what it had once been.

As I turned my back to him and walked slowly across the lobby toward the stairs to the basement, I remembered his boast, "I am the chief because I am the strongest!" that had become only a hollow ring of smoke in the air, with no sound.

The makeshift morgue wasn't cheerful like I remember school. The grownups who were attending the bodies seemed out of place. I'd liked school because everything was in order; there was a reason for everything. If you learned things in order, the way the teacher laid them out, then when you'd finished with a lesson you could see a connection from beginning to end. That was a nice, warm feeling.

When I think about the siege, though, I don't really remember the beginning anymore. It's as if I was born with the shells howling and pounding down on us. They are pieces of metal, with no faces, but they want to kill us. That's hard to accept.

As I stood in the dank schoolroom with its ugly pools of

water that had leaked through the roof, I thought again of the film *Hiroshima Mon Amour*.

But things had changed. I saw myself as being *inside* the film, instead of in the audience watching. The scarred and burned bodies were ones I knew. I could give names to them. The shadow burned on the wall could have been Mother as she went away; I'll never know.

Time and memory had become for me as they were for the woman in the film, something to go in and out of, moving through them with a silent transparency. Perhaps any day now they will come to cut off my hair and lock me in a cellar. I only hope I don't break down and scratch the walls like she did.

Ilija and Dejan and Nenad were beneath the blankets that had been thrown over them. Milorad wasn't with them because he no longer has a face. His face must exist someplace, his mouth that once said proudly, "I'm going to be a chief someday!" only it no longer belonged to his body. It would be out of place for only part of him to be there with the others. They might feel sorry for him, or even laugh, that he never liked. This way he was alone somewhere, but at least he wouldn't be laughed at for not having a face like the others.

That made me feel better for a moment. Looking down at them laid out correctly in a row, their bodies grew in my mind till they almost filled the tiny room. Then I felt my stomach constrict in a cramp, and I became furious at alone, wanting to scream at it and strike it for its uncaring silence. All the alone I'd ever felt rose up in me, and I had to get rid of it.

Just as the grownups started to cover the faces, I ran to a corner and vomited. I was left to myself, perhaps because of the retching sounds that were like a final comment on the still bodies.

I wouldn't have cared if they had looked, though. I was only intent on getting it out of me. I'm sure the others thought I couldn't stand the sight of the dead bodies, but it was for myself that I was grieving. My body chose that method because tears were no longer available to it.

When I'd finished and wiped my mouth on my sleeve, I went back to the bodies and, one after the other, pulled the blankets off their faces. They didn't look so different, a little pale, that's all. Nenad was as quiet in death as he had been in life.

No one tried to stop me. When I got to the end of the line I straightened in a salute, then walked resolutely out of the ruined school. As I passed the silent, unmoving row of living faces, I noticed that they were hardly different than those lying on the floor, only vertical instead of horizontal.

I knew I'd find Luka once again on the stairs when I returned from looking at the bodies. The hotel is his castle and he won't come out now, no matter what, because he doesn't exist outside it.

All the way home all I thought of was facing him. I

HOTEL

thought no more of the bodies, nor of the bloody snow, nor of Milorad's sneaker, but just of Luka's eyes and what I would say to them. I resolved that I'd tell him nothing of what I'd seen. I wouldn't let him use me that way. I couldn't forgive him his quiet acceptance of their fate.

Along the way I saw a man throw away a copy of *Oslobodenje* in disgust. I retrieved it from the trash can and, opening it, counted the black-lined pages. There were four—for Milorad, Dejan, Ilija, and Nenad. Then I stuffed the paper back in the trash can and went on my way.

They were shovelling the red snow away when I reached the Sarajevo. I guess it made them uneasy to just leave it there. They had to feel like there was something they could do.

It was only when my hand touched the door that I realized I'd forgotten to run across Sniper's Alley. That made me smile. I'd defeated the fear of it by not giving in to it, even if it was an oversight.

Inside, the hotel seemed more dark than ever, like it was ashamed of itself. When the door closed behind me, I felt the dark penetrating all the way up inside me. As my eyes adjusted to the dark, I looked around and found the silent, unmoving silhouette of Luka on the stairs. Then I knew that the Sarajevo had become our burial chamber, when once I'd thought it a friend.

The vaults had been constructed out of our own fear. The hotel-tomb reeked of fear. We'd lived in fear, slept with it as it unwittingly raped us all before it destroyed us. We'd bathed with it, when there was water, and eaten it with every bite of food. Eventually there was nothing left of us but fear, and robot eyes to record the horror.

I've chosen black for my drawing. It's really the only possible color if you think about it. How I could ever have considered anything else, even brown or grey, I don't know. That would have minimized the horror, making it easier to bear, and I don't think that's right. If anyone ever sees my drawings, I want them to know what it was really like, even if it makes them throw up.

I didn't realize it until now, watching my hand draw almost by itself, that my drawings have become more abstract. They are no longer real people with real faces, not even an attempt at them, but merely broken lines with frightened circles where eyes and faces used to be. I did one of Adnan, and when I'd finished it was only a stick figure with no legs, looking as if it was begging to be given some. But I couldn't do it. Maybe someone will come along and add them. Then the face will smile again instead of having only a sinkhole for a mouth that can't cry out, "No!" but is only capable of swallowing its horror and its pain until it's full to exploding.

It's only when I draw the pictures that I'm at rest. Then, as soon as I'm finished with one, the need rushes up through me to start another one quickly to keep the chills away. Sometimes, when I look at one I did before, even a few days ago, I wonder, "Who drew that?" Then I remember all too well that I did it myself.

HOTEL

Once I had the idea to draw pictures of before the war. I even started one, but it didn't get very far. I knew right away that it was hopeless.

I'd thought to draw a park and make it happy, with flowers and people. But I only got some broken lines in the foreground that were topped with black circles. I looked at them for a long time before I saw them for what they were. They were flowers—broken, despairing, and ugly. I tore the paper into little pieces as soon as I recognized them. It's not right of me to draw flowers or happy, because now they don't exist for any of us.

My black lines now are making a picture of Milorad and his friends in the snow. My hand is in a fever as it draws. I'm alone in the cellar; the others haven't yet returned from viewing the bodies, and Nihada was left with some neighbors while we were out.

I've taken the blanket down. That's so Luka will be able to see when he comes. I know he'll come because I ripped down the heavy curtains in the lobby, letting in the light. Maybe it was my imagination, but I felt a little warmer, and the sun actually came out from behind its cloud cover to acknowledge me.

Luka will come because the light will drive him here to the dark hole we've been forced to live in and call home. He'll come, too, because he wants to see through my eyes what he can't stand to view through his own.

I've almost finished Milorad's picture. There's a black sun shining, and the hotel is just a quick, savage slash of black in the background. The blood in the snow is also black, of course.

I thought a long time about how to draw Ilija and Dejan and, most of all, Milorad without his head. Then I finally decided the only right thing to do to give them a little dignity was just to draw in their crosses, also black, standing there respectfully where they'd been taken away, so we'd all remember the spot.

Of course they won't be buried there. It's likely they'll be put in the soccer field next to the ice arena from the Olympics. The burial will have to wait until after the sun's gone down. I hope they won't be too cold then.

I'm worried about Milorad's right foot because he left his sneaker in the snow. When I saw it there I thought he'd lost it, but maybe he left it there on purpose, as a reminder.

Luka is here now, looking down at me. I know he's here, even though I don't look up right away. I have to finish the picture first. It's not for Luka anyhow, but for Milorad. There has to be some memory of him.

The picture isn't perfect. It doesn't have the sound of the mute, which is what it's all about, what I started out to draw. Instead of names on the crosses there should be only "ughs," making us all alike. Then anyone who comes here and sees it will know right away that it makes no difference who's buried under each "ugh."

But I won't do it myself. I won't add the "ughs." I've already done as much as I can. Someone else will have to help. That makes me think, "Silly girl, there is no one else!" As Luka said, we're alone.

Still, there's something missing. I can't figure it out at first. I guess Luka's watching makes me nervous. Then, instantly, it's there. Of course, I've forgotten the shells! It's like drawing Christ without his cross. So I put them in—long black streaks raining down on us all, the living and the dead.

Satisfied that I'm finished, I can look up at Luka now. It's not what I'd expected. I thought he'd be pleased too, that I'd completed it.

I've never seen him look frightened before. Now there's a look of absolute terror on his face, like he's been thrown from a car going full speed and is flying head first at a tree that will crush him to pieces.

Now I know why he's gotten so quiet in the last weeks and months. He's been running all the time just like the rest of us, only it's been inside and he couldn't show it, which is the worst running of all. There, no matter how hard or how long you run, you'll always come back to the same place—your own fear. And you'll be left standing in it up to your chin, like an immense pile of your own warm shit that's come to suffocate you.

Luka looks like he's finally stopped running. He's realized it's useless, or he's just tired. Either way, he can barely keep his gaping mouth above the rising shit seeking to drown him.

He wants to say something, but like the mute, he can't get it out. Then finally he does, but it's not a word. It's

SARAJEVO

merely a breath, like a finishing sigh, that's cold and afraid. I have the feeling that if there were no walls around us, it would go on forever, like they say the sound of a wounded whale can travel for thousands of miles in the ocean, searching for its mate.

I'm glad he got it out.

He wants me to draw his picture to make him real, but I can't because I don't see anything when I look at him. There's only the sigh, and I've already found that I can't draw sounds.

I pick up a fresh piece of paper and look down at it silently, away from his accusing eyes. Then when I look up, he's gone.

The next morning Luka went out into the street. I'm the only one who knows why.

He just went, so that he was there when the sniper's bullet came to find him, mercifully.

THE CLOWNS ARE LAUGHING AT ME as they juggle their balloons. Even though they're closed into a glass bubble and surrounded by water, they seem very happy.

Omar has come back.

Our poster is still here, like it was waiting for us to return to it.

Omar said, "I wanted to find them and kill them, but I could not."

He didn't say it at first. It was a long time before he explained things, after we'd made love.

I can tell by the smell that someone has used our mattress since we were here, but I don't mind. I hope they found some comfort here, whoever they were.

How long it's been! Sandra and Milorad and Luka and the others were still alive when we last lay together on this mattress; now they're gone. Of course the porcelain dancer is no longer here because I gave her to Nihada. After Luka was killed, I took Nihada by the hand and led her to a neighbor I knew who'd lost two children of her own. When she opened the door I put Nihada's hand in hers and both of them understood at once. There were tears in the woman's eyes. Nihada actually smiled faintly as she flipped her dancer and watched me go.

I'm glad for Omar, to have him with me. He brought me the clowns, just to make me laugh, he said. I don't know where he got them. When I asked him, he just smiled and said, mysteriously, "magic."

There are two clowns, with big, happy smiles, that I envy, painted on their faces. They've got a lot of balloons between them, and when you shake the bubble, they juggle them for you.

It's some sort of curio. Omar says it's called a water globe. I didn't laugh the first time I saw it, though I was curious. I was sorry for the clowns at being imprisoned under the glass, and wondered how they got there. Then Omar smiled, shaking them and making them juggle before he handed it to me. When I felt the cool of the glass and saw them smiling behind it, I smiled back at them. That made Omar happy. He touched my head, saying, "Your hair is shorter than I remember."

It's true. I cut it the morning Luka went outside to find the sniper's bullet. I was so busy with it I didn't even hear the sound. Or perhaps I did hear it but it just failed to register. After all, it was just one more shot.

I didn't cut my hair for Milorad or Luka or anyone else. I cut it for myself. When Jan failed to recognize me I thought about it, then took out the picture again and thought, "That's not Alma." Right then I decided the hair must go. So it's just a coincidence I cut it after Milorad and the others were killed and Luka went outside. It's

HOTEL

merely the first chance I had. I cut it because I wanted to look like I did before, when Radman and Jan wanted to take me for ice cream. Of course they won't be able to now, because Radman is dead.

I know because I saw his picture in the paper. It was a good likeness, and he was smiling at me, like he used to, when he and Jan were in love.

It was on the Visoko-Zenica highway, near Ticici. The paper didn't say why he was killed, apparently for no reason. They were returning to their hotel and there was no food or supplies in their truck. The gunmen forced them to drive outside town, then shot Radman twice before they took the truck. They shot the other driver too, but he jumped in the Bosna River and swam to safety. When I read the article I wished it had been Radman who'd got away, but then I decided that wasn't right. If my wish could change things, then I'd be responsible for the death of the other driver; so I decided just to remember Radman and miss him. I can't get it out of my head, however, that what put him on that road, at that time, was Jan's slap that said, "Go away!" I hope not, but I can't help thinking about it.

I don't suppose they'll put Radman in the soccer field with Milorad and the others. Since he's French, they'll want to take him home. Then there will be only the memory of his smiling face to remind me that he ever was. I don't know who he was really, except that he was my friend and he bought me ice cream. But at least I know what became of him.

SARAJEVO

I don't know what happened to Luka, how they disposed of him after the sniper's bullet. I didn't go outside to look until they'd taken him away. I left that same morning. When I passed the trash can that had been his throne I wanted to turn it over but I couldn't, so I just walked on without looking back.

I don't know where I went, just wandering in the streets looking at the faces. Then one day, going down one street that was like any other, I heard my name being called. It sounded strange at first, but then I recognized Omar's voice, so I turned to it and welcomed him home.

Omar said there was another globe with a bride and groom and pink flowers, but they looked so solemn and, besides, the inscription said, "The Lord bless and keep you." So he got the clowns because they were laughing and had balloons that he'd always liked. They were like bubbles of happy, he said, as they bounced to and away from the clowns' heads; and it made him laugh to see them.

I wanted to laugh too, and I almost did, watching the reds and blues and yellows of the balloons dancing hypnotically in tiny circles. It had been a long time since I'd seen colors like that. Then I put my face against the glass and felt the hardness and was sorry for the clowns being walled beneath it, even if we could see in and they could see out. But Omar said it was alright, pointing out that they'd be safe there and nothing could come to disturb their smiles. Then I felt better, almost wishing I could be there with them to juggle the balloons with laughter.

HOTEL

Omar must be right, because I've watched them for quite a while and their smiles are still there. There hasn't even been a hint that they'll go away. How happy I am for them!

I wanted to give the clowns names but Omar said no; it was better if we didn't get too attached to them. Of course I see his point. It would have been the same with the cat in the alley on the way home from seeing Jan. If it hadn't scratched me and I'd taken it back to the Sarajevo, then given it a name, it would just have been worse when eventually it went away. When you name a thing or a person it becomes permanent; then when it's lost, the going away is harder to contend with because you're left with the sound of the name burning itself into you. In a way I wish that Milorad and Luka and Mother had not had names at all, or rather, that I didn't know them.

I don't know what to do with the clowns. Omar and I are leaving tomorrow. It's decided. We talked it out without words, sitting on the mattress with our legs beneath us and the clowns smiling between us. When our eyes finished discussing it, we each put a hand over the clowns, protectively, and Omar said, smiling, "There'll be snow tomorrow." I knew what he meant without asking. It will be easier to sneak out of the city with the snow to cover us.

It can be done, he said, even with the mortars set up on the Olympic ski slopes and bobsled runs above the city. Omar knows a path, though it's dangerous. People have

SARAJEVO

been caught and shot there while trying to escape or to bring ammunition and supplies back in. If he were caught, he said, he'd rather be shot on the spot than be held and tortured, and I agreed with him.

He's been on the path before. When he went away just before the end of the summer he braved the path and found his way to Tuzla. He had to go back, he said. Though he had no family left there now, he'd lost his dignity there and he had to try to recover it or live without it and die slowly and horribly, from the inside out, rotting like the gangrene I've seen on some of the victims.

When he told me that, I felt a pain in my chest and wished he'd taken me with him, to find Alma and recover her for myself. Only Omar knew where he'd lost himself and I'm not sure where I lost Alma; that made it easier for him. Though it must have been hard for him going alone.

He kept to himself along the way, he said, staying clear of the roads and eating bark when he could find nothing else. Even so, he was hungry all the time. He had a strange feeling when he entered the outskirts of Tuzla, like going back in time. He imagined for a moment he'd find the little stone house intact. His mother would be inside at the oven making strudel, perhaps even humming as she worked. His sister would come running outside, smiling to coax him into some game. Of course she'd still have her beautiful hair and would never have been raped. He didn't say that, I just added it in my own mind because I could see from his eyes that he wanted it to be so.

Then he found the house. It was hard to locate; every-

209

thing looked different in ruins. Then he was forced to re-live the whole thing. That really scared him, he said, like nothing else before. He sat down on the floor of the little kitchen, collapsing onto its hard comfort.

Everything seemed strange and different. He felt he wasn't really there. There was no Omar in the room; it existed without him. He was shaking, but he couldn't move. After a while he got up and went out of the house.

He never went back. He dragged himself through what was left of the town, just stumbling along without knowing where he was going, until he came to where they were fighting. He could hear their shots, that no longer made him afraid. Almost everyone had cleared out, leaving the soldiers to shoot at one another. Then, strangely, a wrinkled little old man with a bad leg appeared, shuffling out of the rubble of one of the houses, and yelled at him ominously, "You'd better watch out!" before he disappeared just as quickly into another building. Omar paid no attention. Instead, he thought, "If they all kill each other, then there'll be no one left to shoot." We'd all be better off, he told me, without any soldiers. And I agreed with him, except for Radman.

Omar went toward their shots, drawn to them. He came to a low wall and heard a moan, and there was a young soldier lying there at a funny angle with a bloody wound in his side.

When Omar told me that, the thought of Milorad in the snow flashed through my mind, and I wondered if any of the soldier's blood leaked out onto the ground to leave his marker there.

The soldier was trying to crawl to his gun, Omar said. It apparently had been thrown from him when he was hit. There was always the hope that the soldier had thrown it away himself, in disgust, but he wouldn't have been crawling back to it then.

Omar said you could see the sweat on the soldier's face, like wet, running fear, and the fear in his eyes made them wide and bulging. Omar went to the gun and picked it up before the soldier could drag himself there. I found that strange when he told me. As for myself, I'd like to get as far away from any guns as possible. I'm afraid of what I'd want to do with them.

He said the gun felt hard and cold in his hands, not at all like he'd thought. That surprised him; he'd felt it should have been hot from killing. Then he looked up at the soldier's eyes, which, still afraid, were staring intently at him. But what struck Omar then, he said, that he'll never forget, was, "He's afraid of me. He's afraid I'm going to kill him." What a strange new power he felt racing through him! It was all tingly as it washed away the memory of his mother and sister.

He really didn't know how to fire the gun, but to pull the trigger seemed easy. They were so close that when he did put his finger on the trigger he heard a rush of air escaping from the soldier. I thought about that sound, how it would be, and imagined the "ugh" of the deaf mute.

HOTEL

The sound made Omar look closer at the soldier, and he saw how young he was, and how the blood ran silently through his fingers. Perhaps he had a mother or a sister somewhere, alive or dead, and Omar couldn't help wondering about them. He wanted so to believe this was one of the soldiers who'd butchered his own mother and sister, then used him like a cow and left him to cry inwardly at his degradation. He almost shook, he wanted to believe it so badly. But he couldn't force himself to believe it; the face wasn't the same, no matter how hard he tried to make it so in his memory.

The soldier's face relaxed when Omar put down the gun. Then his whole body seemed to relax when Omar sat and watched him, not meanly, but just curiously. In a little while, as the shots got fewer and went farther away, the soldier's breathing got heavier and his eyes started to go blank.

Omar sat and watched him without any emotion at all, until he'd finished dying. Then he got up and walked away out of the town, glad that he wasn't a soldier and didn't know how to fire a gun.

I was glad for him too. I've learned to hate all uniforms.

He came back to Sarajevo, he said, to take me away with him, to the sea, where we'll be safe and happy. It will be easy to get away this time: after all, he did it before, and now we have the snow to help us.

I'm ready to go with him to start a new life. I've never seen the sea, but I'd like to. I imagine the sound of its waves as hospitable, like that of a mother's heart beating against you. I'm old at fourteen, it's true, but I feel there's still time to begin again.

I don't worry about leaving Sarajevo, only it will be hard, I suppose, to get used to the silence without the shells. They've rained down incessantly all day, as though they were telling us good-bye.

They caught some doctors trying to escape and tried them for treason. That worries me a little. I don't see myself as a traitor merely for turning my back on it all, and I don't want to be tried for treason, but then I'm not a doctor. Perhaps leaving is worse for doctors. Anyway, Omar said not to worry about it; we're too insignificant for them to bother with. No one will even notice our absence. Perhaps Clarisse will know and be glad for me. I wish I could take her with me. I could take the clowns but they're a little bulky, and I'm afraid if I slipped and fell they'd break.

I want them to smile and juggle forever, so it's better to leave them here. Maybe when we get to the sea Omar will get me another, with dolphins smiling and leaping through happy waves. When we reach the sea I'm going to run right into it, like greeting a friend.

I don't know if it will be warm there or not, or if there will be palm trees, like in the poster of Pleasure Island. I didn't think to ask Omar before he fell asleep, and I don't want to bother him with it now. Details aren't important. We'll be together and we'll have our happiness between us, like the clowns have their balloons. That's all that counts.

With my eyes closed I picture us there on the beach. I

can see it clearly but there's no sound, like a silent movie. I'm smiling and running, only not away from anything but to Omar, whose smile is waiting to receive me.

I can see our happiness. It's all around, radiating from us like heat waves rising off our bodies as we run to one another. How beautiful it is to feel yourself sweat, and to see and then feel the sweat from the body of one you love and know it's not from fear! Then when we come together, our sweat will merge, and there'll be no secrets to keep, ever.

We'll start from scratch. Everything will be new and different. We won't have to duck our heads when we run and, if we don't feel like it, we won't run at all. We'll walk leisurely along hand in hand, watching sunrises and sunsets. They'll be the same to us, and we won't worry about the end of one day because there will always be another to replace it.

And after we've watched our sunset and made love, we won't have to go to sleep hungry, either. There'll be plenty of food there just for the taking. Omar will fish, and I'll collect coconuts.

I suppose after a while we'll want to make some sort of shelter. I won't want it to be right on the beach, but perhaps on a little hill overlooking the sea so we can see far away, and the sunlight dancing off the waves will be like the balloons when the clowns juggle them.

I want to take something with me when we go, to put in our new house. I thought about it and decided on the picture of myself I drew for Jan. It's not perfect, I know,

SARAJEVO

otherwise she wouldn't have rejected it. That's why I'm still working on it. But when I've got it just right and there's a smile on her face, then I'll present it to Omar, coming out proudly to surprise him. How happy he'll be! He'll not toss it away, I'm sure. He'll quit what he's doing right away and, holding the picture high like a trophy, bear it triumphantly back to our house to tack on the wall.

I'm proud that he returned for me and wants me to go with him. I know I can be a help to him when he needs me. I'm strong, and not afraid of work. It's true there're many things I'm ignorant about—geography and cooking for instance—but I feel I can learn if given the chance. I remember some things from watching Mother in the kitchen, and Omar will teach me about the world. Together we'll make do.

It makes me happy when Omar wants me; I'm a part of him then. Still, though, I'm newly surprised each time he comes to me. Today he was soft and gentle. I closed my eyes and imagined myself a flower. His hands were gentle winds blowing against me, and I swayed with their caresses. I tried hard to imagine the sounds of the shells as thunder, not harsh, but distant and muted, as though they were bringing a spring rain. His kisses were wet, and I pretended the rain had come and was washing me all over. How happy I was to receive it! My face was smiling as I turned it up to him to be kissed again and again.

The rain slackened on my face, then stopped. The thunder went farther away, merely a dying growl, and then it stopped as well.

HOTEL

It was quite some time, lying there beneath Omar's sweating, resting body, feeling his heart beat like the thunder, before I realized the shelling had stopped. I expected it to start up again at any time. That's all my ears could listen for. I was glad when his heart calmed and he rolled quietly off me to go to sleep, so I could listen more easily for the explosions and be ready for them when they first began.

But something strange happened, or rather, nothing happened. They didn't start again. Even after a long time of listening—nothing. Perhaps it's just some short truce and they haven't told anyone yet. By the time we get the news it'll have started again, so there'll be no real rest at all.

But now I decide, with Omar soundly asleep next to me, not to worry about it, to enjoy the quiet while I can. I reach for the clowns, carefully so as not to disturb Omar. They must be glad to see me because right away they're smiling and juggling as soon as I give them a shake. I suppose they'll be sad to be left behind and want to play a little now while there's time.

Suddenly I feel a little strange, uncomfortable, and I don't know why. Something's wrong; it's as though I don't belong here. My whole body feels strange. I've got the twitches and can't keep still. I'm jerking about so, I'm afraid I'll wake Omar. Everything seems weird—the poster, the room, everything. The mattress must have bugs, it's making me so jumpy.

Trying to settle things down, I hold the clowns tightly

216

in both hands and let them rest on my chest. But they're still smiling and juggling, more energetically than ever! I look to see if Omar notices anything, but he's sound asleep. Nothing ever wakes him.

I'm all itchy, jumping around inside myself, and I don't know what to do about it. The clowns aren't any help, their nervous energy constantly reminding me of my own agitation. So I set them on the floor next to the mattress and instantly they stop juggling and just stand there smiling with the balloons falling around them. Then I pick them up again and immediately they're at it like mad.

In the gathering dark I hold the clowns against me until my hands stop shaking and they can rest. There's no question of leaving them behind now. I'll find a place for them somewhere.

If it hadn't been for them I'd never have discovered how afraid I've been all along. Without their juggling balloons I'd never have seen my own hands shaking, and then accepted the fact of my trembling heart and the almost epileptic convulsions of my lips.

I'm not ashamed, though I once would have been. I only wonder how long I've been shaking, and if anyone else noticed. If they did, it was nice of them not to tell me. They probably couldn't see my shaking for their own.

I'm not sure I'd have wanted to know before. It's only now with the quiet that I'm able to identify my fear, to admit it to myself, and to face it.

I've always been afraid. I was afraid just a little while ago when Omar held me. Even with his kisses I con-

HOTEL

stantly had an ear out for the shells, afraid they'd take me away like Milorad, and I'd never even know it. I wasn't even able to totally appreciate the love I was given because of the fear I couldn't even recognize.

Now I know that the fear has been the worst of all. It's a shaky, sickening fear that makes you want to throw up, and you don't even know why, because you've trained yourself not to feel.

I was afraid to see Milorad dead, glad that they'd taken him away, preferring instead to feel nothing. I was afraid to go into the street until they'd removed Luka's body, and I didn't even know it.

I was afraid when we buried Sandra.

I was afraid when Omar left and when he returned—perhaps it would happen again.

I was afraid in the raid on the gardens.

I was afraid of Mira, and for her.

I was afraid to enter Mother's room in the deserted flat, not wanting to find her, to find a body and have to admit that she hadn't just "gone away" but was dead.

When I first came to the Sarajevo I'd been afraid of not being accepted.

I was even afraid of the dead lovers in the sanctuary, though I had to go see them.

Before the war, I can see it now, I was afraid of Mother's silence.

I was afraid most of all that I'd never be loved because I was plain.

Now it's finished. I hope so and I believe so. I'm not

SARAJEVO

shaking anymore. There's not a smile on my face yet, but I can feel one beginning inside, as I snuggle close to the back of Omar to accept the warmth of him. I'm all through with ducking my head and being ashamed.

I reach over Omar to put the clowns on a shelf so I can see them smiling while I fall off to sleep. The quiet is my friend, and so are the clowns who showed me my fear, because next time I'll be able to give myself completely to love and not worry about whether the shells are coming for us. I can't stop them from coming, but I can defeat them by rejecting my fear of them.

The quiet I feel now is the quiet of my heart, and I'm not afraid of tomorrow.

THE SIGN SAYS, in large, black, frenzied letters on a white background, "Beware! Sniper!" Against the backdrop of the snow we must resemble the twisted, agonizing scrawls, only they can't escape. They're bound by the limits of the sign, and we're leaving.

The clowns are happy that we're going, and also happy that I didn't leave them behind.

Omar didn't see me when I stuffed them in my bag. Hanging back, I waited until he'd already gone outside in the dark before hurriedly popping them into the already full knapsack. They gave me a smile, and I smiled back at them. Omar called, "Hurry, Alma!" and I rushed out to him, giving him a quick kiss before he had time to complain.

There was no one about as we made our way toward the river. When the light started to come I was shocked to see the buildings. While we were committed to staying, I'd never viewed them as ruins. But now, on leaving, *Hiroshima Mon Amour* came to mind again, and my eyes were forced to admit the desolation was real. I was glad not to have to say good-bye to the Sarajevo. I don't want to remember it like that. I'd like to remember the courtyard as

SARAJEVO

a happy place, with Milorad and Luka laughing under the sycamore, not the fact that Sandra is buried there. But to just push it aside makes little of all our effort and suffering, so I don't know which is better, remembering or forgetting. Probably I'll have to make do with a little of each.

The morning I left the hotel, after Luka was killed, there was a loud noise from the courtyard. I didn't go back to look, but I heard on the street that the sycamore had just cracked, almost straight down the middle, then toppled over. It was a horrible tearing, crashing, finishing noise when it crashed to the ground, like a dying breath. Some said it was because of age. Others, that it must have been hit once, just slightly, which now caused it to keel over. But I knew it just got tired of supporting itself in the face of it all, and so gave up, like Mira leaning against the wall of her kiosk.

I didn't go back to look because I want to remember it tall and proud, with all our names emblazoned on it, not lying on its side, sad and defeated. In a way I'm sorry now that I rubbed my name out with the spoon.

I know I'll remember I loved Luka once, and why. I know now how weak and afraid I was when I first came to the Sarajevo, no matter what my face or my words said. Then Luka was strong. I don't know if he was lying too, only that we felt strength flowing from him to us, and that we'd never have made it without him. He held us together, whether he planned it or not, and gave us a reason to be. Without that we'd all probably have been like Mira long ago, at the very start, and I wouldn't have the nerve to leave now. I guess at the end his strength was just used up. He'd given all he had to us and then there was suddenly none left to sustain him. We'd become more while he'd become less. And, once he saw he didn't exist anymore as Luka, he chose to go outside instead.

I can see I'll have to be very careful about what I choose to remember and what to forget. I want to remember Mother in some way, but I haven't decided how. Not just as silence.

Of course there's Clarisse—how to forget her! I'll always recall the happy closeness of touching noses with her, and looking into her eyes.

I'll remember Kemal's eyes as well. If we all had eyes like that, unable to see another's differences and defects, then none of this would ever have happened. Perhaps Kemal and Clarisse were the happiest of all.

I won't forget Mira either. I'm glad I was there for her at the end. I wasn't there for Milorad, but he must have known that I loved him, else I wouldn't have allowed him to pester me each time he needed to feel close. I hope that the end came so fast for him that he didn't have time to be alone. That's the way it must have been for the shadow people on the walls in the Hiroshima film. I don't know if that was real or just a film, but this is real, believe me.

I don't think I want to forget anything. To forget is to deny, and that can only make you shake inside, then slowly rot if you don't get it out. Better to bear it proudly, like a badge of honor, with our heads held high, and remember we were Sarajevans.

SARAJEVO

"Hurry, Alma!" Omar is calling again. He's nearly across the intersection on his way to the bridge. I run after him, not because I'm afraid, but simply to catch up. He smiles when I reach him.

It's the Cumuriza Bridge over the Miljacka, in the middle of the city. It was heavily damaged early in the war, but the steel girders are still there, like a stubborn skeleton that refuses to go away, and they look strong now in the early light.

They are the beginning of our road to safety, to freedom, and to the sea that will greet me, I know, with open arms.

When we reach the edge of the bridge Omar takes my arm, then pushes me ahead of him onto the long sidebeam that is our highway across. I think he figures it's safer to get across first, that the longer you're exposed the more dangerous it is. Frankly, I don't see that it makes any difference. They could get you from the back as well as from the front, or even from the side.

We're not alone in going. A few others are there before us. There's a young boy just in front of me. I can't see his face, only his white breath rising in the cold air. In front of him there's a woman carrying a child. She's got him under one arm, to the side, with her other hand steadying herself on the railing. I can see his face. He peeks out at me with wide eyes from beneath a large cap and hood, and when I smile at him he smiles back. He probably thinks they're only on the way to market and he's going to get something tasty once there, baklava perhaps. I wonder where they're going and hope they'll travel a little way with us.

Omar told me the whole plan. Once across the river we'll go through the new district till we're close to the front lines. Then we'll wait for night to fall before we sneak through. He says we can breathe easy once we get through the lines. They won't expect to find us in back of them. The only danger then will be from wandering patrols. We'll have to keep a close eye out for them, especially when we're skirting the airport. After that we'll head for the foothills of Mount Igman, then south toward Mostar and the sea. I can't wait to begin our life together there!

I have confidence in Omar's direction, and will follow his lead. I'm strong and no longer afraid, and he knows I'm here for him when he needs me. We haven't much in our knapsacks, it's true, only a change of clothes, a loaf of bread each (Omar swiped them from the market yesterday), and some tins of meat—I don't know what kind, the labels have come off. In any case, we'll manage. Omar has a knife. He found it in the ruins of Tuzla and thoughtfully brought it along. Then there are the clowns in case we need to laugh.

I almost slip on the wet railing and Omar catches me. It's good to have his arm around me, supporting me. I'd like to lean back against him, luxuriating in the comfort, but there's no time for that.

There's a *ping!* somewhere ahead against the steel of

SARAJEVO

the bridge, that makes the woman pull the child closer to her and duck her head. I don't duck, so Omar pushes my head down for me. When I manage to free myself and pull away I give him a furious look that says, "Don't do that again!" He seems to understand.

We get across the bridge without any more shots being fired, thanks to the snow I suppose. That was easier than I'd thought! It was almost as easy as I imagine it would be to climb the gangplank to the blue ship bound for Pleasure Island.

As soon as I step off onto solid ground again I look back across the skeleton bridge and almost expect to see Milorad and the rest tagging along behind through the rising mist. Then Omar coughs and I know they won't be coming.

When I turn back I see the woman and the child have taken another way. That makes me sad. Now there are only the clowns to keep us company.

It's just as Omar said. On our way through the district toward the lines no one pays us any attention. Their own private emergencies are written across their faces, like they've been trampled on and they carry the footprints as creases and wrinkles. They simply have no time to bother with us. It feels good to be lost among them. When we reach the sea we'll have plenty of time to make friends. We'll invite them to our house, where I'll cook the fish that Omar will catch.

We continue to hear occasional shots ahead of us.

HOTEL

When the shots get really loud so we know they're close, Omar picks an abandoned building to shelter us for a few hours until it's dark. It's not so good as "our house," as there's no poster or mattress, but it'll do. Omar sits against the wall so he can look out, and I sit next to him, waiting for the dark. He doesn't say anything and I don't either, but we're both intensely aware of the other's presence. I hope my breathing is as slow and even as his, and that he can't hear my heart thumping between the shooting. Perhaps he does, because he takes my hand in his, and I'm glad for its company.

It's a good thing the dark comes early now. The waiting is worse than the going. Our hands were together almost the whole time, until it was like they were growing together. The only interruption was when Omar got up and went to the back to relieve himself. Even then his hand hesitated a moment in letting go, as though he wanted to take mine with him. I was cold without him, but I had to smile when I heard him pissing against the wall. I waited till he was finished to get up and do my own, and then I came back and our hands found each other again and stayed together till it was dark.

Now his hand tugs mine as he rises, and I know it's time.

Outside, the dark is complete. The snow must have gone away with the day. It can't be far to the front lines. Omar's hand still has mine as we go forward. In the shadowy dark every building is like a ghost that we're saying

226

SARAJEVO

good-bye to. With their torn walls and roofs they look sad and mournful to see us go. We're luckier than they. They're planted here, stuck, with no way to escape. It makes me feel a little guilty to slip silently among them on our way out. Their windows are like pathetic, longing eyes, and after a while I can't look at them but only concentrate on Omar's back ahead of me.

It's strange to be going away; Sarajevo is all I've known. But I don't think about that, only about our future together and where it will lead us.

It's quiet now in the night without the shooting, and there's nothing until we come to the end of a row of buildings. Then we're in the open for a second, and there's a barricade in front of us with voices on the other side. I think, "They're the enemy," and I want to tell Omar, but he quickly puts his hand over my mouth.

We're invisible in the darkness, but as we move along the barricade that separates us from them, I catch a little of what they're saying.

One voice, young and hopeful, says, "She'll wait for me, I'm sure. She's a good girl."

On down the line, disjointed, another, huskier voice replies, "We've waited so long now, my ass is frozen." I stifle a laugh; I've felt that way myself.

Later, a frightened voice seems to be talking to itself, "I haven't heard from Mother . . ." That makes me sad.

It seems right that we should call out and go over and talk to them, but Omar's hand pulling me away says no. When we come to a break in the wire, he hesitates for a

227

moment before he darts through, plucking me after him and hurriedly pulling me down behind a tree. I feel his breath coming in short, hot gasps on my face and realize I should be afraid.

I'd really like to look at the faces of the voices to see if they're different from us, but I know it's impossible. It would be senseless to even mention it. It's possible, I know, that they're the ones who hurt Adnan, or Omar; that one of them launched the mortar that blew off Milorad's head, or even that one is the soldier with hairy hands who took me on Zuc. Still, I have trouble imagining them as criminals from the sound of their voices, and wish I could tell them of my own mother and my own waiting. Perhaps we're all criminals for letting things happen, even just by giving our silent assent.

When we leave the last buildings behind and start to climb a hill away from the city, there are no more voices, so I think, relieved, "Is that all there is to getting away?" It's so simple we could have done it long ago.

I'm happy with the steep climb through the trees, happy with my body exerting itself in going away, and I'm not tired at all when we get to the top. Omar wants to rest for a second, and we look back down at the whiteness covering the rooftops of the city. I'm dizzy like I'm on a ferris wheel that's come to the very top. I want to hang there forever and never have it come down!

But it does come down, because Omar starts resolutely down the other side of the hill that, when we've descended, will block the city from us. Then it will be like the voices, and I'll have to think very hard to believe it really existed.

I want to leave something there on the hill, to watch over the city and remember it for me so I won't have to, not all of it anyway. So, quickly, without losing sight of Omar, I take out the clowns and put them safely in the hollow of a stump. Then I hurry and catch up to Omar, taking his hand. I look back to see if the clowns are still smiling, and they are.

It wasn't hard getting around the airport. We made a wide circle through the thick woods, like a hike almost. Omar tried to make it a game, calling out quietly under his breath, "your left . . . left, right, left," and I found myself silently laughing, trying to match his cadence.

Once, through the trees, I could see the runways. They seemed like long lines to nowhere. I could imagine the planes landing and taking off, but I couldn't imagine myself on one of them. If I had lost a leg or an eye it would have been different. You had to be wounded to deserve a place there, and we'd gotten away completely unharmed. From the looks of us, we'd gotten away clean.

At the end of the first night, just before dawn, we came out of the woods into a meadow. Omar stopped, and there was a sound that couldn't have been his. He moved aside and there was a cow standing there watching us, like she was lost and glad to see us. I went toward her and she mooed again and I touched her nose, and she tossed her head like she was happy for my touch. I was happy, too, that I'd found a friend, and I made Omar touch her as well, even though he was reluctant. But then she mooed for him and tried to nuzzle him, and that made him smile.

We were both sorry to leave her there in the middle of the clearing. She looked after us and mooed and then started to follow, so that Omar had to chuck a rock after her to make her go back. She still looked after us as we disappeared into the trees. I hope she'll be alright.

With the morning, it started to snow again. But Omar decided that even with the snow we shouldn't be about too long in the light. He cut some branches with his knife and arranged them under a large fir tree, like a pallet, but so you couldn't tell anything was out of the ordinary by looking from the outside. He made me test it to see before I came under the tree with him.

We must be somewhere in the foothills of Mount Igman, he said, and tonight we'll go around it. In a few days things will be safer, and we'll be on our way to the sea.

We ate some of the bread and, proud of himself for his night's work, Omar said we'd celebrate, and he opened one of the tins of meat with his knife.

After we ate, he lay down to sleep and I lay next to him to keep him warm, and that's all I remember until the sound of the planes.

They're droning somewhere high overhead, like gigantic bees buzzing in the dark. At first I think they're a dream, but then the cold takes hold of me and I see the snow and know they're real.

I've always thought snow is more beautiful at night than in the day. There's something inviting about it. It seems fragile but luminous all at once, and the dark of the sky forms a protective canopy over it, like the glass dome over the clowns. Now I know why they're always smiling and will juggle whenever you ask them to. They feel safe under their dome, knowing that nothing bad will ever happen to them there. The worst would be if someone dropped them and their dome broke, spilling them out onto the ground like dying fish thrown onto the land. I don't like to imagine them lying there helpless on their sides. But they'd probably never consider the possibility until it happened, and then it would be over before the smiles even had a chance to leave their faces.

Omar awakens sleepily, rubbing his eyes and looking like one of the clowns, so that I'd like to juggle snowballs with him. But when he hears the planes, he remembers where he is and jumps up to go.

The branches have made a warm bed, and I'm sorry to leave them. Perhaps someone else will find them and be happy that we've prepared a bed for them.

Omar brushes the snow off himself and then off of me. I'm like a big doll he's stroking, and that feels so good.

He points upward to where the planes are still buzzing. Somehow our excursion has been invested with the power of silence. It's a great secret between us that we're

HOTEL

headed to the sea. Gestures are okay, but words are not allowed. Too many of them would spoil everything.

Then we're out from under our tree and Omar starts
off manfully across the snow, sinking with every step,
looking like some intrepid explorer out to conquer his own
private mountain. I'm happy for his footsteps, making the
going easier as I scramble along behind him.

During the night I don't think about much except his
footsteps and keeping up with him. When I'm cold, I
allow myself briefly to think of the sea, to imagine its
sunny warmth and picture the blue of its friendly, lapping
waves coming to greet us.

The planes are like a friend too. For a while their happy
sounds keep us company. They're like bees directing us to
the hive. Then their buzzing diminishes, going away, and
they're gone. I'm sorry to hear them go. It's hard to tell the
exact time of when they are and when they're not, so I listen for a long time before my ears give up. Then there's
only the quiet, broken by the sound of Omar struggling in
the snow. I can hear his struggle, but I don't feel my own,
and I don't know I'm tired until it starts to get light.

Omar sits on a log for a rest, with me close beside. As
soon as our bodies quit walking, I know we must have
come a long way in the night. And I think, "We're that
much closer to the sea." Omar looks at me brightly, as
though he has a secret to share. He reaches into his sock
to pull out a piece of tinfoil, containing two squares of
chocolate that he's saved. His eyes invite me to have one,

SARAJEVO

and it tastes sweet and wonderful, like I'm lying in the sand and someone is dropping dates into my open mouth.

I want to run ahead so we'll reach the sea faster, so I bounce off the log and my laughter says for him to follow. A door opens in my mind, that was closed before, and for a second I don't know what it is. Then I hear the hills throwing my laughter back at me, laughing with me, and I realize it's been so long that I'd forgotten the freedom of a laugh, and how it runs happily through you like you're being washed by a crystal flowing spring.

Omar's voice calls out, "Alma!" that is also laughter, that makes me want to run again, and I do.

I'm running through the trees to the sea with Omar's laughing voice after me. There's nothing else. I have no arms or legs even. There's just his laughter pursuing me and pushing me on.

Then his laughter stops, and I stop and turn to look for it. He's gone to examine something in the snow. I go to him, happily, to share in what he's found.

It's food! and clothes and toys even, that are wrapped in plastic and scattered about over the side of the hill, like Christmas has come early and they've been thrown from a sleigh. Then I understand: the planes came in the night to bring us gifts, and I look up to thank them.

Omar is wild with excitement that he doesn't have words for, but his happy smiles are enough. He breaks open some of the packages and stuffs his pockets and then the knapsack. It's a while before we've got everything we can carry. Then, even loaded down, I don't feel burdened at all. Something blows across the hill, *whoosh!* that makes us both jump. Then we laugh. It's the parachute that brought us presents. It must have broken free from the trees and now is blowing away, and I run with it, like with laughter. For a minute I'm floating free and happy, like the parachute. Then there's something else in the snow that makes me stop.

It's a Raggedy Ann looking just like Clarisse, so I want to call out to her. But, picking her up, it's not Clarisse because she's still got both arms. Turning to Omar to show her off, like presenting a newborn baby to the father, I decide she can be a new Clarisse, the Clarisse of our journey to the sea. I'm happy to see that Omar accepts her also.

In a minute we're a family. I cradle baby Clarisse in my arms and hum to her a little so she'll get to know the sound of my voice. Omar hums as well, breaking off a stick to use as a staff while making a trail. He shoulders the stick like a pretend gun and calls back to me in cadence, "your left . . . your left, right, left," that makes me laugh out loud again—how good it feels!—as I try to keep pace with him.

We're in the trees, and then we're out of them. Then Omar stops abruptly on "your left," so when his voice breaks off I'm stuck laughing on one foot.

I look up from my laughing feet to Omar's face, then beyond Omar to the soldier, and my laughter dies quickly within me, like it had never been.

H IS NAME IS GORAN, and he's all smiles, joking with the others. His unit calls themselves "Panthers." He takes off his cap and brushes back his dark hair, then laughs and rubs his hands against the cold.

Their breaths are rising steam in the pre-dawn air, as is mine, but I don't feel the cold. I'm hoping the sun will come in a moment, and that it will rise quickly. I can't say a prayer for that, but I hope for it greatly. There's a hint of dawn, so there's a chance.

Omar is sitting on the ground next to me, quite close. I've been standing since they led the others away and then we heard the shots. The sound of them is not really scary if you don't think about it. Not scary, anyway, like the screams of the burning woman running from the Hotel Bristol, or sitting on Adnan's bed where his legs should have been, or the mute's "ugh." Those things had made me want to throw up. The sound of the shots was crisp and clean in the cold air, and could have been hunting.

After the shots and then a pause, Goran and the other soldiers came back out of the woods laughing and congratulating one another.

I heard Goran say he'd soon be back shooting pool at

HOTEL

the VBC, and another smiled and said he wanted to ski on Mount Jahorina.

I've never done either of those things, and now I never will.

We know Goran's name because it was he who found us when we came out of the trees.

That was yesterday, though it seems longer. When we looked up and saw him, Omar dropped the stick off his shoulder, bravely but uselessly, like it was a gun. But I saw the defeat in the sag of his shoulders. The soldier's gun was real and we were trapped in the open like rabbits with no place to run. I hugged new Clarisse to me a little before I dropped her in the snow.

Goran seemed proud he'd found us when he brought us back to the others. We've had a chance to talk since then. He offered us each some chocolate. Omar didn't take his, but I did mine and thanked Goran for it, not subserviently but just plainly, as Mother taught me.

Goran likes my picture, the one I drew of myself, or rather was going to finish when I had the chance. It still needs some work, I think, but Goran said no, it's fine the way it is. Perhaps Mother would have liked it also, I don't know.

When Goran's searching hand found the drawing inside my coat, it brushed against my breast. I could feel it lingering there, not knowing exactly what to do. It didn't make me feel good, like when Milorad was excited to see me in the shower, nor did it leave me flat and cold as the soldier on Zuc did when he took me. I just accepted that

236

his hand would linger there and didn't give it any thought whatsoever. It didn't concern me. It was his hand, and he'd have to worry about it.

Then, after his eyes thought about it, Goran's hand went away without holding me there. I suppose I liked him for that, though it makes no difference anymore. His hand held up the drawing for the others to see, and he smiled and said "an artist." It didn't give me any satisfaction to hear him say it because I'm not completely satisfied with it myself. Then he asked me would I do one of him, for a girl, but I said no. That made him stop smiling, but in a little while he got over it and was joking with his friends again.

Omar wasn't ready, I guess, when they led the other prisoners away, because he squeezed my hand. I don't know if it was involuntary, or if he wanted to tell me something privately.

They were scared, the other two—an old man and a young soldier. The young one should not have been scared because he was a soldier, but then I thought, "That's no excuse; he's like anyone else," so I didn't think badly of him when he cried a little.

The old man didn't cry. His face was calm, but his hands were shaking. I hoped Goran wouldn't be one of those to take him into the woods, but he was. Then I was glad I'd said no when he asked me to do the picture.

The soldiers who didn't take the others into the trees didn't pay them any mind. Some of them prepared breakfast out of their tins and boxes on top of a fallen log. I watched their faces carefully and they didn't even jump when the shots were fired.

Omar didn't jump either, but he squeezed my hand again, so that I knew now that he was talking to me. His hand wasn't saying good-bye, however, but was talking fast to tell me about the blue of the sea I'd never seen.

His hand is still talking to me as he rises when Goran and the others come toward us. And I'm listening, feverishly, so that I can't hear anything else.

Goran's eyes are excited, but not mean, as they lead us toward the trees.

I can feel the momentary stiffness in Omar's body as we walk, that is resistance. But his hand begins talking to me again, and I'm trying so hard to get everything he's saying that there's no room for anything else.

He's telling me, without reserve, of the blue, blue, blue of the sea that stretches on forever, and of the sun that will warm us there. It will be so hot, his hand says, that we'll be too lazy to want anything but an occasional dip in the lapping waves, and we'll never have to be cold again.

I'm there with him on the beach, listening to his hand, warm all over, not wanting or needing anything but his presence . . . Then he tumbles in the snow and I'm instantly cold as the beach is replaced by images of Luka laughing on his trash can throne, and Milorad's sneaker in the snow, and then of the young girl in Adnan's hospital room as she tried in vain to reach her tiny doll for comfort. I never knew if she lived or died, but I remember her nonetheless, a sister.

238

SARAJEVO

Omar struggles to rise, his hand talking fast again.

Then we're with the soldiers among the hiding trees.

Omar's hand says, hotly, "Remember me," and mine answers back, "Yes."

The soldiers are together in a short line and Goran pushes us ahead of and away from them before he goes back to the others.

Goran calls out for us to step apart, but Omar's hand hasn't finished talking to me, so I shake my head "no."

I don't look at Omar and he doesn't look at me, but his hand is talking faster now, nervously, so that it's a little hard to make everything out, though I catch "blue" very distinctly each time he says it.

Avoiding the eyes of the soldiers, I raise mine to the horizon, toward Sarajevo, where we had moments of happiness that must last us.

Then, as I hear the metallic clicking of their laughing rifles, I go in my mind to my room in the Sarajevo, feeling its comfort.

I want to be buried beneath the sycamore tree in the courtyard with Omar next to me, and with Luka and Sandra and Milorad and the rest all around, friends. But I know in my heart we will be left here, alone.

Then I think of the dead lovers in the sanctuary, how they fell together, and suddenly I'm not concerned anymore and, smiling, I let my eyes meet their killing ones, and in the knowledge I see there of my bravery and acceptance I find myself for the first time, the very first, beautiful, and I squeeze Omar's hand to tell him so.

HOTEL

Just before they shoot, a bird flies calling overhead, be-yond the trees, not in despair but in expectation, and I imagine myself thusly, going toward the new sun . . .

The sun rises swiftly, gently kissing the tops of the trees with its warmth, like a smile, or a promise.